# Gris Grimly's
# TALES from the BROTHERS GRIMM

# Gris Grimly's
# Tales from the Brothers Grimm

Being a selection from the Household Stories
collected by

Jacob and Wilhelm Grimm

Translated from the German by
MARGARET HUNT

And done into pictures by
Gris Grimly

NEW YORK: BALZER + BRAY
HarperCollins*Publishers*
MMXVI

Balzer + Bray is an imprint of HarperCollins Publishers.

Gris Grimly's Tales from the Brothers Grimm


---

Library of Congress Cataloging-in-Publication Data
Grimm, Jacob, 1785-1863.
[Kinder- und Hausmärchen. Selections. English]
Gris Grimly's tales from the brothers Grimm : being a selection from the Household Stories collected by Jacob and Wilhelm Grimm / translated from the German by Margaret Hunt and done into pictures by Gris Grimly.
pages cm
Summary: An illustrated collection of forty traditional tales collected by the Grimm brothers.
ISBN 978-0-06-235233-0 (hardcover : alk. paper)
1. Fairy tales—Germany. [1. Fairy tales. 2. Folklore—Germany.] I. Grimm, Wilhelm, 1786-1859. II. Hunt, Alfred William, Mrs., 1831-1912 translator. III. Grimly, Gris, illustrator. IV. Title.
PZ8.G882Gy 2015 2014039005
398.20943—dc23 CIP
AC

---

16 17 18 19 20 CG/RRDH 10 9 8 7 6 5 4 3 2 1
Typography by Dana Fritts
Hand lettering by Leah Palmer Preiss

First Edition

*For Lynnette*

# TABLE OF CONTENTS

# The Frog King, or Iron Henry

N OLD TIMES WHEN WISHING STILL HELPED ONE, there lived a king whose daughters were all beautiful, but the youngest was so beautiful that the sun itself, which has seen so much, was astonished whenever it shone in her face. Close by the king's castle lay a great dark forest, and under an old linden tree in the forest was a well; and when the day was very warm, the king's child went out into the forest and sat down by the side of the cool fountain; and when she was dull, she took a golden ball and threw it up on high and caught it, and this ball was her favorite plaything.

Now it so happened that on one occasion the princess's golden ball did not fall into the little hand which she was holding up for it, but onto the ground beyond and rolled straight into the water. The king's daughter followed it with her eyes, but it vanished; and the well was deep, so deep that the bottom could not be seen. On this she began to cry, and cried louder and louder, and could not be comforted. And as she thus lamented someone said to her, "What ails thee, king's daughter? Thou weepest so that even a stone would show pity."

She looked round to the side from whence the voice came, and saw a frog stretching forth its thick, ugly head from the water. "Ah! old water-splasher, is it thou?" said she. "I am weeping for my golden ball, which has fallen into the well."

"Be quiet, and do not weep," answered the frog. "I can help thee, but what wilt thou give me if I bring thy plaything up again?"

"Whatever thou wilt have, dear frog," said she, "my clothes, my pearls and jewels, and even the golden crown which I am wearing."

The frog answered, "I do not care for thy clothes, thy pearls and jewels, or thy golden crown, but if thou wilt love me and let me be thy companion and playfellow and sit by thee at thy little table, and eat off thy little golden plate and drink out of thy little cup, and sleep in thy little bed—if thou wilt promise me this, I will go down below and bring thee thy golden ball up again."

"Oh, yes," said she. "I promise thee all thou wishest, if thou wilt but bring me my ball back again." She, however, thought, "How the silly frog does talk! He lives in the water with the other frogs, and croaks, and can be no companion to any human being!"

But the frog, when he had received this promise, put his head into the water and sank down, and in a short while came swimming up again with the ball in his mouth and threw it on the grass. The king's daughter was delighted to see her pretty plaything once more, and picked it up and ran away with it. "Wait, wait," said the frog. "Take me with thee. I can't run as thou canst." But what did it avail him to scream his croak, croak after her, as loudly as he

could? She did not listen to it, but ran home and soon forgot the poor frog, who was forced to go back into his well again.

The next day when she had seated herself at table with the king and all the courtiers, and was eating from her little golden plate, something came creeping—splish splash, splish splash—up the marble staircase; and when it had got to the top, it knocked at the door and cried, "Princess, youngest princess, open the door for me." She ran to see who was outside, but when she opened the door, there sat the frog in front of it. Then she slammed the door to, in great haste, sat down to dinner again, and was quite frightened.

The king saw plainly that her heart was beating violently, and said, "My child, what art thou so afraid of? Is there perchance a giant outside who wants to carry thee away?"

"Ah, no," replied she. "It is no giant but a disgusting frog."

"What does a frog want with thee?"

"Ah, dear father, yesterday as I was in the forest sitting by the well, playing, my golden ball fell into the water. And because I cried so, the frog brought it out again for me, and because he so insisted, I promised him he should be my companion, but I never thought he would be able to come out of his water! And now he is outside there, and wants to come in to me."

In the meantime, it knocked a second time, and cried,

*"Princess! youngest princess!*
*Open the door for me!*
*Dost thou not know what thou saidst to me*
*Yesterday by the cool waters of the fountain?*
*Princess, youngest princess!*
*Open the door for me!"*

Then said the king, "That which thou hast promised must thou perform. Go and let him in."

She went and opened the door, and the frog hopped in and followed her, step by step, to her chair. There he sat and cried, "Lift me up beside thee." She delayed, until at last the king commanded her to do it. When the frog was once on the chair, he wanted to be on the table, and when he was on the table, he said, "Now, push thy little golden plate nearer to me that we may eat together." She did this, but it was easy to see that she did not do it willingly. The frog enjoyed what he ate, but almost every mouthful she took choked her. At length he said, "I have eaten and am satisfied. Now I am tired: carry me into thy little room and make thy little silken bed ready, and we will both lie down and go to sleep."

The king's daughter began to cry, for she was afraid of the cold frog which she did not like to touch, and which was now to sleep in her pretty, clean little bed. But the king grew angry and said, "He who helped thee when thou wert in trouble ought not afterwards to be despised by thee."

So she took hold of the frog with two fingers, carried him upstairs, and put him in a corner. But when she was in bed, he crept to her and said, "I am tired. I want to sleep as well as thou. Lift me up or I will tell thy father." Then she was terribly angry, and took him up and threw him with all her might against the wall.

"Now, thou wilt be quiet, odious frog," said she. But when he fell down, he was no frog but a king's son with beautiful kind eyes. He by her father's will was now her dear companion and husband. Then he told her how he had been bewitched by a wicked witch, and how no one could have delivered him from the well but herself, and that tomorrow they would go together into his

IRON HENRY

kingdom. Then they went to sleep, and next morning when the sun awoke them, a carriage came driving up with eight white horses, which had white ostrich feathers on their heads and were harnessed with golden chains, and behind stood the young king's servant Iron Henry.

Iron Henry had been so unhappy when his master was changed into a frog that he had caused three iron bands to be laid round his heart, lest it should burst with grief and sadness. The carriage was to conduct the young king into his kingdom. Iron Henry helped them both in, and placed himself behind again, and was full of joy because of this deliverance. And when they had driven a part of the way, the king's son heard a cracking behind him as if something had broken. So he turned round and cried, "Henry, the carriage is breaking."

"No, master, it is not the carriage. It is a band from my heart, which was put there in my great pain when you were a frog and imprisoned in the well." Again and once again while they were on their way something cracked, and each time the king's son thought the carriage was breaking; but it was only the bands which were springing from the heart of Iron Henry because his master was set free and was happy.

# Cat and Mouse in Partnership

A CERTAIN CAT HAD MADE THE ACQUAINTANCE OF A mouse, and had said so much to her about the great love and friendship she felt for her that at length the mouse agreed that they should live and keep house together. "But we must make a provision for winter, or else we shall suffer from hunger," said the cat, "and you, little mouse, cannot venture everywhere, or you will be caught in a trap someday."

The good advice was followed, and a pot of fat was bought, but they did not know where to put it. At length, after much consideration, the cat said, "I know no place where it will be better stored up than in the church, for no one dares take anything away from there. We will set it beneath the altar, and not touch it until we are really in need of it." So the pot was placed in safety, but it was not long before the cat had a great yearning for it, and said to the mouse, "I want to tell you something, little mouse; my cousin has brought a little son into the world, and has asked me to be godmother; he is white with brown spots, and I am to hold him over the font at the christening. Let me go out today, and you look after the house by yourself."

"Yes, yes," answered the mouse, "by all means go, and if you get anything very good, think of me. I should like a drop of sweet red christening wine, too." All this, however, was untrue; the cat had no cousin and had not been asked to be godmother. She went straight to the church, stole to the pot of fat, began to lick at it, and licked the top of the fat off. Then she took a walk upon the roofs of the town, looked out for opportunities, and then stretched herself in the sun and licked her lips whenever she thought of the pot of fat; and not until it was evening did she return home. "Well, here you are again," said the mouse. "No doubt you have had a merry day."

"All went off well," answered the cat.

"What name did they give the child?"

"Top-off!" said the cat quite coolly.

"Top-off!" cried the mouse. "That is a very odd and uncommon name. Is it a usual one in your family?"

"What does it signify?" said the cat. "It is no worse than Crumb-stealer, as your godchildren are called."

Before long the cat was seized by another fit of longing. She said to the mouse, "You must do me a favour, and once more manage the house for a day alone. I am again asked to be godmother, and, as the child has a white ring round its neck, I cannot refuse." The good mouse consented, but the cat crept behind the town walls to the church, and devoured half the pot of fat. "Nothing ever seems so good as what one keeps to oneself," said she, and was quite satisfied with her day's work.

When she went home the mouse inquired, "And what was this child christened?"

"Half-done," answered the cat.

"Half-done! What are you saying? I never heard the name in my life, I'll wager anything it is not in the calendar!"

The cat's mouth soon began to water for some more licking. "All good things go in threes," said she. "I am asked to stand godmother again. The child is quite black, only it has white paws, but with that exception, it has not a single white hair on its whole body; this only happens once every few years. You will let me go, won't you?"

"Top-off! Half-done!" answered the mouse. "They are such odd names, they make me very thoughtful."

"You sit at home," said the cat, "in your dark-grey fur coat and long tail, and are filled with fancies—that's because you do not go out in the daytime."

During the cat's absence the mouse cleaned the house and put it in order, but the greedy cat entirely emptied the pot of fat. "When everything is eaten up, one has some peace," said she to herself, and well filled and fat she did not return home till night.

The mouse at once asked what name had been given to the third child. "It will not please you more than the others," said the cat. "He is called All-gone."

"All-gone," cried the mouse, "that is the most suspicious name of all! I have never seen it in print. All-gone; what can that mean?" And she shook her head, curled herself up, and lay down to sleep.

From this time forth no one invited the cat to be godmother, but when the winter had come and there was no longer anything to be found outside, the mouse thought of their provision, and said, "Come, cat, we will go to our pot of fat which we have stored up for ourselves—we shall enjoy that."

"Yes," answered the cat, "you will enjoy it as much as you would enjoy sticking that dainty tongue of yours out of the window." They set out on their way, but when they arrived, the pot of fat certainly was still in its place, but it was empty. "Alas!" said the mouse. "Now I see what has happened, now it comes to light! You are a true friend! You have devoured all when you were standing godmother. First top off, then half done, then—"

"Will you hold your tongue," cried the cat. "One word more and I will eat you, too."

"All gone" was already on the poor mouse's lips; scarcely had she spoken it before the cat sprang on her, seized her, and swallowed her down. Verily, that is the way of the world.

# Faithful John

HERE WAS ONCE ON A TIME AN OLD KING WHO WAS ill, and thought to himself, "I am lying on what must be my deathbed." Then said he, "Tell Faithful John to come to me." Faithful John was his favorite servant, and was so called because he had for his whole life long been so true to him. When therefore he came beside the bed, the king said to him, "Most faithful John, I feel my end approaching and have no anxiety except about my son. He is still of tender age and cannot always know how to guide himself. If thou dost not promise me to teach him everything that he ought to know, and to be his foster father, I cannot close my eyes in peace."

Then answered Faithful John, "I will not forsake him, and will serve him with fidelity, even if it should cost me my life."

On this, the old king said, "Now I die in comfort and peace." Then he added, "After my death, thou shalt show him the whole castle: all the chambers, halls, and vaults, and all the treasures which lie therein, but the last chamber in the long gallery, in which is the picture of the princess of the Golden Dwelling, shalt thou not show. If he sees that picture, he will fall violently in love with her and will drop down in a swoon and go through great danger for her sake; therefore thou must preserve him from that." And when Faithful John had once more given his promise to the old king about this, the king said no more but laid his head on his pillow and died.

When the old king had been carried to his grave, Faithful John told the young king all that he had promised his father on his deathbed, and said, "This will I assuredly perform and will be faithful to thee as I have been faithful to him, even if it should cost me my life." When the mourning was over, Faithful John said to him, "It is now time that thou shouldst see thine inheritance. I will show thee thy father's palace." Then he took him about everywhere, up and down, and let him see all the riches and the magnificent apartments; only there was one room which he did not open, that in which hung the dangerous picture. The picture was, however, so placed that when the door was opened, you looked straight on it; and it was so admirably painted that it seemed to breathe and live, and there was nothing more charming or more beautiful in the whole world.

The young king, however, plainly remarked that Faithful John always walked past this one door, and said, "Why dost thou never open this one for me?"

"There is something within it," he replied, "which would terrify thee."

But the king answered, "I have seen all the palace, and I will know what is in this room also," and he went and tried to break open the door by force.

Then Faithful John held him back and said, "I promised thy father before his death that thou shouldst not see that which is in this chamber; it might bring the greatest misfortune on thee and on me."

"Ah, no," replied the young king. "If I do not go in, it will be my certain destruction. I should have no rest day or night until I had seen it with my own eyes. I shall not leave the place now until thou hast unlocked the door."

Then Faithful John saw that there was no help for it now, and with a heavy heart and many sighs, sought out the key from the great bunch. When he had opened the door, he went in first, and thought by standing before him he could hide the portrait so that the king should not see it in front of him; but what availed that? The king stood on tiptoe and saw it over his shoulder. And when he saw the portrait of the maiden, which was so magnificent and shone with gold and precious stones, he fell fainting to the ground. Faithful John took him up, carried him to his bed, and sorrowfully thought, "The misfortune has befallen us. Lord God, what will be the end of it?" Then he strengthened him with wine, until he came to himself again.

The first words the king said were, "Ah, the beautiful portrait! Whose is it?"

"That is the princess of the Golden Dwelling," answered Faithful John.

Then the king continued, "My love for her is so great that if all the leaves on all the trees were tongues, they could not declare it. I will give my life to win her. Thou art my most Faithful John, thou must help me."

The faithful servant considered within himself for a long time how to set about the matter, for it was difficult even to obtain a sight of the king's daughter. At length he thought of a way, and said to the king, "Everything which she has about her is of gold—tables, chairs, dishes, glasses, bowls, and household furniture. Among thy treasures are five tons of gold; let one of the goldsmiths of the kingdom work these up into all manner of vessels and utensils, into all kinds of birds, wild beasts, and strange animals, such as may please her, and we will go there with them and try our luck."

The king ordered all the goldsmiths to be brought to him, and they had to work night and day until at last the most splendid things were prepared. When everything was stowed on board a ship, Faithful John put on the dress of a merchant, and the king was forced to do the same in order to make himself quite unrecognizable. Then they sailed across the sea, and sailed on until they came to the town wherein dwelt the princess of the Golden Dwelling.

Faithful John bade the king stay behind on the ship and wait for him. "Perhaps I shall bring the princess with me," said he. "Therefore see that everything is in order; have the golden vessels set out and the whole ship decorated." Then he gathered together in his apron all kinds of gold things, went on shore, and walked straight to the royal palace.

When he entered the courtyard of the palace, a beautiful girl was standing there by the well with two golden buckets in her hands, drawing water with them. And when she was just turning round to carry away the sparkling water, she saw the stranger and asked who he was. So he answered, "I am a merchant," and opened his apron and let her look in.

Then she cried, "Oh, what beautiful gold things!" and put her pails down and looked at the golden wares one after the other. Then said the girl, "The princess must see these; she has such great pleasure in golden things that she will buy all you have." She took him by the hand and led him upstairs, for she was the waiting-maid.

When the king's daughter saw the wares, she was quite delighted and said,

"They are so beautifully worked that I will buy them all of thee."

But Faithful John said, "I am only the servant of a rich merchant. The things I have here are not to be compared with those my master has in his ship. They are the most beautiful and valuable things that have ever been made in gold." She wanted to have everything brought to her there, but he said, "There are so many of them that it would take a great many days to do that, and so many rooms would be required to exhibit them that your house is not big enough."

Then her curiosity and longing were still more excited, until at last she said, "Conduct me to the ship. I will go there myself and behold the treasures of thine master."

On this Faithful John was quite delighted and led her to the ship; and when the king saw her, he perceived that her beauty was even greater than the picture had represented it to be and thought no other than that his heart would burst in twain. Then she got into the ship, and the king led her within. Faithful John, however, remained behind with the pilot and ordered the ship to be pushed off, saying, "Set all sail till it fly like a bird in air." Within, however, the king showed her the golden vessels, every one of them, also the wild beasts and strange animals.

Many hours went by whilst she was seeing everything, and in her delight she did not observe that the ship was sailing away. After she had looked at the last, she thanked the merchant and wanted to go home, but when she came to the side of the ship, she saw that it was on the deep sea far from land, and hurrying onwards with all sail set. "Ah," cried she in her alarm, "I am betrayed! I am carried away and have fallen into the power of a merchant—I would die rather!"

The king, however, seized her hand, and said, "I am not a merchant. I am a king, and of no meaner origin than thou art; and if I have carried thee away with subtlety, that has come to pass because of my exceeding great love for thee. The first time that I looked on thy portrait, I fell fainting to the ground." When the princess of the Golden Dwelling heard that, she was comforted, and her heart was inclined unto him, so that she willingly consented to be his wife.

It so happened, however, while they were sailing onwards over the deep sea, that Faithful John, who was sitting on the forepart of the vessel, making music, saw three ravens in the air, which came flying towards them. On this he stopped playing and listened to what they were saying to one another, for that he well understood. One cried, "Oh, there he is carrying home the princess of the Golden Dwelling."

"Yes," replied the second, "but he has not got her yet."

Said the third, "But he has got her; she is sitting beside him in the ship."

Then the first began again and cried, "What good will that do him? When they reach land, a chestnut horse will leap forward to meet him, and the prince will want to mount it; but if he does that, it will run away with him and rise up into the air with him, and he will never see his maiden more."

Spake the second, "But is there no escape?"

"Oh, yes, if anyone else gets on it swiftly and takes out the pistol, which must be in its holster, and shoots the horse dead with it, the young king is saved. But who knows that? And whosoever does know it, and tells it to him, will be turned to stone from the toe to the knee."

Then said the second, "I know more than that: even if the horse be killed, the young king will still not keep his bride. When they go into the castle together, a wrought bridal garment will be lying there in a dish and looking as if it were woven of gold and silver. It is, however, nothing but sulfur and pitch; and if he put it on, it will burn him to the very bone and marrow."

Said the third, "Is there no escape at all?"

"Oh, yes," replied the second. "If anyone with gloves on seizes the garment and throws it into the fire and burns it, the young king will be saved. But what avails that? Whosoever knows it and tells it to him, half his body will become stone from the knee to the heart."

Then said the third, "I know still more: even if the bridal garment be burnt, the young king will still not have his bride. After the wedding, when the dancing begins and the young queen is dancing, she will suddenly turn pale and fall down as if dead; and if someone does not lift her up and draw three drops of blood from her right breast and spit them out again, she will die. But if anyone who knows that were to declare it, he would become stone from the crown of his head to the sole of his foot."

When the ravens had spoken of this together, they flew onwards, and Faithful John had well understood everything; but from that time forth he became quiet and sad, for if he concealed what he had heard from his master, the latter would be unfortunate, and if he discovered it to him, he himself must sacrifice his life. At length, however, he said to himself, "I will save my master, even if it bring destruction on myself."

When therefore they came to shore, all happened as had been foretold by the ravens, and a magnificent chestnut horse sprang forward. "Good," said the king, "he shall carry me to my palace," and was about to mount it when Faithful John got before him, jumped quickly on it, drew the pistol out of the holster, and shot the horse.

Then the other attendants of the king, who after all were not very fond of Faithful John, cried, "How shameful to kill the beautiful animal that was to have carried the king to his palace."

But the king said, "Hold your peace and leave him alone; he is my most faithful John, who knows what may be the good of that!" They went into the palace, and in the hall there stood a dish, and therein lay the bridal garment looking no otherwise than as if it were made of gold and silver. The young king went towards it and was about to take hold of it, but Faithful John pushed him away, seized it with gloves on, carried it quickly to the fire, and burnt it.

The other attendants again began to murmur, and said, "Behold, now he is even burning the king's bridal garment!"

But the young king said, "Who knows what good he may have done; leave him alone, he is my most faithful John."

And now the wedding was solemnized: the dance began, and the bride also took part in it. Then Faithful John was watchful and looked into her face; and suddenly she turned pale and fell to the ground as if she were dead. On this he ran hastily to her, lifted her up, and bore her into a chamber—then he laid her down and knelt and sucked the three drops of blood from her right breast, and spat them out.

Immediately she breathed again and recovered herself, but the young king had seen this, and being ignorant why Faithful John had done it, was angry and cried, "Throw him into a dungeon."

Next morning Faithful John was condemned and led to the gallows, and when he stood on high and was about to be executed, he said, "Everyone who has to die is permitted before his end to make one last speech; may I too claim the right?"

"Yes," answered the king, "it shall be granted unto thee."

Then said Faithful John, "I am unjustly condemned, and have always been true to thee"; and he related how he had hearkened to the conversation of the ravens when on the sea, and how he had been obliged to do all these things in order to save his master.

Then cried the king, "Oh, my most Faithful John. Pardon, pardon—bring him down." But as Faithful John spoke the last word he had fallen down lifeless and become a stone.

Thereupon the king and the queen suffered great anguish, and the king said, "Ah, how ill I have requited great fidelity!" and ordered the stone figure to be taken up and placed in his bedroom beside his bed. And as often as he looked on it, he wept and said, "Ah, if I could bring thee to life again, my most faithful John."

Some time passed and the queen bore twins, two sons who grew fast and were her delight. Once when the queen was at church and the two children were sitting playing beside their father, the latter full of grief again looked at the stone figure, sighed, and said, "Ah, if I could but bring

thee to life again, my most faithful John."

Then the stone began to speak and said, "Thou canst bring me to life again if thou wilt use for that purpose what is dearest to thee."

Then cried the king, "I will give everything I have in the world for thee."

The stone continued, "If thou wilt cut off the heads of thy two children with thine own hand and sprinkle me with their blood, I shall be restored to life."

The king was terrified when he heard that he himself must kill his dearest children, but he thought of faithful John's great fidelity and how he had died for him, drew his sword, and with his own hand cut off the children's heads.

And when he had smeared the stone with their blood, life returned to it, and Faithful John stood once more safe and healthy before him. He said to the king, "Thy truth shall not go unrewarded," and took the heads of the children, put them on again, and rubbed the wounds with their blood, on which they became whole again immediately and jumped about and went on playing as if nothing had happened. Then the king was full of joy, and when he saw the queen coming, he hid Faithful John and the two children in a great cupboard.

When she entered, he said to her, "Hast thou been praying in the church?"

"Yes," answered she, "but I have constantly been thinking of Faithful John and what misfortune has befallen him through us."

Then said he, "Dear wife, we can give him his life again, but it will cost us our two little sons, whom we must sacrifice."

The queen turned pale, and her heart was full of terror, but she said, "We owe it to him, for his great fidelity."

Then the king was rejoiced that she thought as he had thought, and went and opened the cupboard and brought forth Faithful John and the children, and said, "God be praised; he is delivered, and we have our little sons again also," and told her how everything had occurred. Then they dwelt together in much happiness until their death.

# Our Lady's Child

ARD BY A GREAT FOREST DWELT A WOOD-CUTTER with his wife, who had an only child, a little girl three years old. They were so poor, however, that they no longer had daily bread and did not know how to get food for her. One morning the wood-cutter went out sorrowfully to his work in the forest; and while he was cutting wood, suddenly there stood before him a tall and beautiful woman with a crown of shining stars on her head, who said to him, "I am the Virgin Mary, mother of the child Jesus. Thou art poor and needy; bring thy child to me. I will take her with me and be her mother and care for her."

The wood-cutter obeyed, brought his child, and gave her to the Virgin Mary, who took her up to heaven with her. There the child fared well, ate sugar-cakes and drank sweet milk; and her clothes were of gold, and the little angels played with her. And when she was fourteen years of age, the Virgin Mary called her one day and said, "Dear child, I am about to make a long journey, so take into thy keeping the keys of the thirteen doors of heaven. Twelve of these thou mayest open, and behold the glory which is within them, but the thirteenth, to which this little key belongs, is forbidden thee. Beware of opening it, or thou wilt bring misery on thyself." The girl promised to be obedient, and when the Virgin Mary was gone, she began to examine the dwellings of the kingdom of heaven. Each day she opened one of them, until she had made the round of the twelve. In each of them sat one of the apostles in the midst of a great light, and she rejoiced in all the magnificence and splendor, and the little angels who always accompanied her rejoiced with her.

Then the forbidden door alone remained, and she felt a great desire to know what could be hidden behind it, and said to the angels, "I will not quite open it, and I will not go inside it, but I will unlock it so that we can just see a little through the opening."

"Oh no," said the little angels, "that would be a sin. The Virgin Mary has forbidden it, and it might easily cause thee unhappiness." Then she was silent, but the desire in her heart was not stilled but gnawed there and tormented her and let her have no rest.

And once when the angels had all gone out, she thought, "Now I am quite alone, and I could peep in. If I do it, no one will ever know." She sought out the key, and when she had got it in her hand, she put it in the lock; and when she had put it in, she turned it round as well. Then the door sprang open, and she saw there the Trinity sitting in fire and splendor. She stayed there awhile, and looked at everything in amazement; then she touched the light a little with her finger, and her finger became quite golden. Immediately a great fear fell

on her. She shut the door violently and ran away. Her terror, too, would not quit her, let her do what she might; and her heart beat continually and would not be still. The gold, too, stayed on her finger and would not go away, let her rub it and wash it ever so much.

It was not long before the Virgin Mary came back from her journey. She called the girl before her, and asked to have the keys of heaven back. When the maiden gave her the bunch, the Virgin looked into her eyes and said, "Hast thou not opened the thirteenth door also?"

"No," she replied.

Then she laid her hand on the girl's heart, and felt how it beat and beat, and saw right well that she had disobeyed her order and had opened the door. Then she said once again, "Art thou certain that thou hast not done it?"

"Yes," said the girl, for the second time.

Then she perceived the finger which had become golden from touching the fire of heaven, and saw well that the child had sinned, and said for the third time "Hast thou not done it?"

"No," said the girl for the third time.

Then said the Virgin Mary, "Thou hast not obeyed me, and besides that, thou hast lied; thou art no longer worthy to be in heaven."

Then the girl fell into a deep sleep, and when she awoke she lay on the earth below and in the midst of a wilderness. She wanted to cry out, but she could bring forth no sound. She sprang up and wanted to run away, but whithersoever she turned herself, she was continually held back by thick hedges of thorns through which she could not break. In the desert, in which she was imprisoned, there stood an old hollow tree, and this had to be her dwelling place. Into this she crept when night came, and here she slept. Here, too, she found a shelter from storm and rain, but it was a miserable life, and bitterly did she weep when she remembered how happy she had been in heaven and how the angels had played with her. Roots and wild berries were her only food, and for these she sought as far as she could go. In the autumn she picked up the fallen nuts and leaves and carried them into the hole. The nuts were her food in winter; and when snow and ice came, she crept amongst the leaves like a poor little animal that she might not freeze. Before long her clothes were all torn; and one bit of them after another fell off her. As soon, however, as the sun shone warm again, she went out and sat in front of the tree, and her long hair covered her on all sides like a mantle. Thus she sat year after year, and felt the pain and the misery of the world.

One day, when the trees were once more clothed in fresh green, the king of the country was hunting in the forest and followed a roe; and as it had fled into the thicket which shut in this part of the forest, he got off his horse, tore the bushes asunder, and cut himself a path with his sword. When he had at last forced his way through, he saw a wonderfully beautiful maiden sitting under the tree; and she sat there and was entirely covered with her golden hair down to her very feet. He stood still and looked at her full of surprise, then he spoke to her and said, "Who art thou? Why art thou sitting here in the wilderness?" But she gave no answer, for she could not open her mouth. The king continued, "Wilt thou go with me to my castle?" Then she just nodded her head a little. The king took her in his arms, carried her to his horse, and rode home with her; and when he reached the royal castle, he caused her to be dressed in beautiful garments and gave her all things in abundance. Although she could not speak, she was still so beautiful and charming that he began to love her with all his heart, and it was not long before he married her.

After a year or so had passed, the queen brought a son into the world. Thereupon the Virgin Mary appeared to her in the night when she lay in her bed alone, and said, "If thou wilt tell the truth and confess that thou didst unlock the forbidden door, I will open thy mouth and give thee back thy speech, but if thou perseverest in thy sin and deniest obstinately, I will take thy newborn child away with me."

Then the queen was permitted to answer, but she remained hard and said, "No, I did not open the forbidden door"; and the Virgin Mary took the newborn child from her arms and vanished with it.

Next morning when the child was not to be found, it was whispered among the people that the queen was a man-eater and had killed her own child. She heard all this and could say nothing to the contrary, but the king would not believe it, for he loved her so much.

When a year had gone by, the queen again bore a son, and in the night the Virgin Mary again came to her, and said, "If thou wilt confess that thou openedst the forbidden door, I will give thee thy child back and untie thy tongue; but if you continuest in sin and deniest it, I will take away with me this new child also."

Then the queen again said, "No, I did not open the forbidden door"; and the Virgin took the child out of her arms, and away with her to heaven.

Next morning, when this child also had disappeared, the people declared quite loudly that the queen had devoured it, and the king's councillors demanded that she should be brought to justice. The king, however, loved her so dearly that he would not believe it and commanded the councillors under pain of death not to say any more about it.

The following year the queen gave birth to a beautiful little daughter, and for the third time the Virgin Mary appeared to her in the night and said, "Follow me." She took the queen by the hand and led her to heaven, and showed her there her two eldest children, who smiled at her and were playing with the ball of the world. When the queen rejoiced thereat, the Virgin Mary said, "Is thy heart not yet softened? If thou wilt own that thou openedst the forbidden door, I will give thee back thy two little sons."

But for the third time the queen answered, "No, I did not open the forbidden door." Then the Virgin let her sink down to earth once more and took from her likewise her third child.

Next morning, when the loss was reported abroad, all the people cried loudly, "The queen is a man-eater. She must be judged," and the king was no longer able to restrain his councillors. Thereupon a trial was held, and as she could not answer and defend herself, she was condemned to be burnt alive. The wood was got together, and when she was fast bound to the stake, and the fire began to burn round about her, the hard ice of pride melted, her heart was moved by repentance, and she thought, "If I could but confess before my death that I opened the door." Then her voice came back to her, and she cried out loudly, "Yes, Mary, I did it"; and straightaway rain fell from the sky and extinguished the flames of fire, and a light broke forth above her, and the Virgin Mary descended with the two little sons by her side, and the newborn daughter in her arms.

She spoke kindly to her, and said, "He who repents his sin and acknowledges it is forgiven." Then she gave her the three children, untied her tongue, and granted her happiness for her whole life.

# The Story of the Youth Who Went Forth to Learn What Fear Was

CERTAIN FATHER HAD TWO SONS, THE ELDER OF whom was smart and sensible and could do everything, but the younger was stupid and could neither learn nor understand anything; and when people saw him, they said, "There's a fellow who will give his father some trouble!"

When anything had to be done, it was always the elder who was forced to do it; but if his father bade him fetch anything when it was late or in the night-time, and the way led through the churchyard or any other dismal place, he answered, "Oh, no, Father, I'll not go there; it makes me shudder!" for he was afraid.

Or when stories were told by the fire at night which made the flesh creep, the listeners sometimes said, "Oh, it makes us shudder!"

The younger sat in a corner and listened with the rest of them and could not imagine what they could mean. "They are always saying, 'It makes me shudder, it makes me shudder!' It does not make me shudder," thought he. "That, too, must be an art of which I understand nothing."

Now it came to pass that his father said to him one day, "Hearken to me, thou fellow in the corner there, thou art growing tall and strong, and thou, too, must learn something by which thou canst earn thy living. Look how thy brother works, but thou dost not even earn thy salt."

"Well, Father," he replied, "I am quite willing to learn something—indeed, if it could but be managed, I should like to learn how to shudder. I don't understand that at all yet."

The elder brother smiled when he heard that, and thought to himself, "Good God, what a blockhead that brother of mine is! He will never be good for anything as long as he lives. He who wants to be a sickle must bend himself betimes."

The father sighed and answered him, "Thou shalt soon learn what it is to shudder, but thou wilt not earn thy bread by that."

Soon after this the sexton came to the house on a visit, and the father bewailed his trouble and told him how his younger son was so backward in every respect that he knew nothing and learnt nothing. "Just think," said he, "when I asked him how he was going to earn his bread, he actually wanted to learn to shudder."

"If that be all," replied the sexton, "he can learn that with me. Send him to me, and I will soon polish him."

The father was glad to do it, for he thought, "It will train the boy a little."

The sexton therefore took him into his house, and he had to ring the bell.

After a day or two, the sexton awoke him at midnight and bade him arise and go up into the church tower and ring the bell. "Thou shalt soon learn what shuddering is," thought he, and secretly went there before him; and when the boy was at the top of the tower and turned round and was just going to take hold of the bell rope, he saw a white figure standing on the stairs opposite the sounding hole.

"Who is there?" cried he, but the figure made no reply, and did not move or stir. "Give an answer," cried the boy, "or take thyself off; thou hast no business here at night."

The sexton, however, remained standing motionless that the boy might think he was a ghost. The boy cried a second time, "What do you want here? Speak if thou art an honest fellow, or I will throw thee down the steps!"

The sexton thought, "He can't intend to be as bad as his words," uttered no sound, and stood as if he were made of stone. Then the boy called to him

for the third time; and as that was also to no purpose, he ran against him and pushed the ghost down the stairs, so that it fell down ten steps and remained lying there in a corner. Thereupon he rang the bell, went home, and without saying a word went to bed and fell asleep.

The sexton's wife waited a long time for her husband, but he did not come back. At length she became uneasy and wakened the boy and asked, "Dost thou not know where my husband is? He climbed up the tower before thou didst."

"No, I don't know," replied the boy, "but someone was standing by the sounding hole on the other side of the steps, and as he would neither give an answer nor go away, I took him for a scoundrel and threw him downstairs; just go there and you will see if it was he. I should be sorry if it were."

The woman ran away and found her husband, who was lying, moaning in the corner, and had broken his leg.

She carried him down, and then with loud screams she hastened to the boy's father. "Your boy," cried she, "has been the cause of a great misfortune! He has thrown my husband down the steps and made him break his leg. Take the good-for-nothing fellow away from our house."

The father was terrified, and ran thither and scolded the boy. "What wicked tricks are these?" said he. "The devil must have put this into thy head."

"Father," he replied, "do listen to me. I am quite innocent. He was standing there by night like one who is intending to do some evil. I did not know who it was, and I entreated him three times either to speak or to go away."

"Ah," said the father, "I have nothing but unhappiness with you. Go out of my sight. I will see thee no more."

"Yes, Father, right willingly. Wait only until it is day. Then will I go forth and learn how to shudder, and then I shall, at any rate, understand one art which will support me."

"Learn what thou wilt," spake the father, "it is all the same to me. Here are fifty thalers for thee. Take these and go into the wide world, and tell no one from whence thou comest and who is thy father, for I have reason to be ashamed of thee."

"Yes, Father, it shall be as you will. If you desire nothing more than that, I can easily keep it in mind."

When day dawned, therefore, the boy put his fifty thalers into his pocket and went forth on the great highway, and continually said to himself, "If I could but shudder! If I could but shudder!"

Then a man approached who heard this conversation which the youth was holding with himself, and when they had walked a little farther to where they could see the gallows, the man said to him, "Look, there is the tree where seven men have married the rope maker's daughter and are now learning how to fly. Sit down below it, and wait till night comes, and you will soon learn how to shudder."

"If that is all that is wanted," answered the youth, "it is easily done; but if I learn how to shudder as fast as that, thou shalt have my fifty thalers. Just come back to me early in the morning." Then the youth went to the gallows, sat down below it, and waited till evening came. And as he was cold, he lighted himself a fire, but at midnight the wind blew so sharply that in spite of his fire, he could not get warm. And as the wind knocked the hanged men against each other, and they moved backwards and forwards, he thought to himself, "Thou shiverest below by the fire, but how those up above must freeze and suffer!" And as he felt pity for them, he raised the ladder and climbed up,

unbound one of them after the other, and brought down all seven. Then he stirred the fire, blew it, and set them all round it to warm themselves. But they sat there and did not stir, and the fire caught their clothes. So he said, "Take care, or I will hang you up again." The dead men, however, did not hear, but were quite silent and let their rags go on burning. On this he grew angry, and said, "If you will not take care, I cannot help you. I will not be burnt with you," and he hung them up again each in his turn. Then he sat down by his fire and fell asleep.

The next morning the man came to him and wanted to have the fifty thalers, and said, "Well, dost thou know how to shudder?"

"No," answered he, "how was I to get to know? Those fellows up there did not open their mouths, and were so stupid that they let the few old rags which they had on their bodies get burnt."

Then the man saw that he would not get the fifty thalers that day, and went away saying, "One of this kind has never come my way before."

The youth likewise went his way, and once more began to mutter to himself, "Ah, if I could but shudder! Ah, if I could but shudder!"

A wagoner who was striding behind him heard that and asked, "Who are you?"

"I don't know," answered the youth.

Then the wagoner asked, "From whence comest thou?"

"I know not."

"Who is thy father?"

"That I may not tell thee."

"What is it that thou art always muttering between thy teeth?"

"Ah," replied the youth, "I do so wish I could shudder, but no one can teach me how to do it."

"Give up thy foolish chatter," said the wagoner. "Come, go with me, I will see about a place for thee."

The youth went with the wagoner, and in the evening they arrived at an inn where they wished to pass the night. Then at the entrance of the room the youth again said quite loudly, "If I could but shudder! If I could but shudder!"

The host, who heard this, laughed and said, "If that is your desire, there ought to be a good opportunity for you here."

"Ah, be silent," said the hostess. "So many inquisitive persons have already lost their lives—it would be a pity and a shame if such beautiful eyes as these should never see the daylight again."

But the youth said, "However difficult it may be, I will learn it, and for this purpose indeed have I journeyed forth." He let the host have no rest, until the latter told him that not far from thence stood a haunted castle where anyone could very easily learn what shuddering was, if he would but watch in it for three nights. The king had promised that he who would venture should have his daughter to wife, and she was the most beautiful maiden the sun shone on. Great treasures likewise lay in the castle, which were guarded by evil spirits, and these treasures would then be freed and would make a poor man rich enough. Already many men had gone into the castle, but as yet none had come out again.

Then the youth went next morning to the king and said if he were allowed, he would watch three nights in the haunted castle. The king looked at him, and, as the youth pleased him, he said, "Thou mayest ask for three things to take into the castle with thee, but they must be things without life."

Then he answered, "Then I ask for a fire, a turning lathe, and a cutting board with the knife." The king had these things carried into the castle for him during the day.

When night was drawing near, the youth went up and made himself a bright fire in one of the rooms, placed the cutting-board and knife beside it, and seated himself by the turning-lathe. "Ah, if I could but shudder!" said he, "but I shall not learn it here either."

Towards midnight he was about to poke his fire, and as he was blowing it, something cried suddenly from one corner, "Au, miau! how cold we are!"

"You simpletons!" cried he. "What are you crying about? If you are cold, come and take a seat by the fire and warm yourselves." And when he had said that, two great black cats came with one tremendous leap and sat down on each side of him and looked savagely at him with their fiery eyes.

After a short time, when they had warmed themselves, they said, "Comrade, shall we have a game at cards?"

"Why not?" he replied. "But just show me your paws." Then they stretched out their claws. "Oh," said he, "what long nails you have! Wait, I must first cut them for you." Thereupon he seized them by the throats, put them on the cutting-board, and screwed their feet fast. "I have looked at your fingers," said he, "and my fancy for card playing has gone," and he struck them dead and threw them out into the water. But when he had made away with these two, and was about to sit down again by his fire, out from every hole and corner came black cats and black dogs with red-hot chains; and more and more of them came until he could no longer stir, and they yelled horribly and got on his fire, pulled it to pieces, and tried to put it out.

He watched them for a while quietly, but at last when they were going too far, he seized his cutting-knife, and cried, "Away with ye, vermin," and began to cut them down. Some of them ran away; the others he killed and threw out into the fishpond. When he came back he fanned the embers of his fire again and warmed himself. And as he thus sat, his eyes would keep open no longer, and he felt a desire to sleep. Then he looked round and saw a great bed in the corner. "That is the very thing for me," said he, and got into it. When he was just going to shut his eyes, however, the bed began to move of its own accord, and went over the whole of the castle. "That's right," said he, "but go faster." Then the bed rolled on as if six horses were harnessed to it, up and down, over thresholds and steps, but suddenly—hop, hop—it turned over upside down and lay on him like a mountain. But he threw quilts and pillows up in the air, got out, and said, "Now anyone who likes may drive," and lay down by his fire, and slept till it was day.

In the morning the king came, and when he saw him lying there on the ground, he thought the evil spirits had killed him and he was dead. Then said he, "After all, it is a pity—he is a handsome man."

The youth heard it, got up, and said, "It has not come to that yet."

Then the king was astonished, but very glad, and asked how he had fared. "Very well indeed," answered he. "One night is past; the two others will get over likewise."

Then he went to the innkeeper, who opened his eyes very wide and said, "I never expected to see thee alive again! Hast thou learnt how to shudder yet?"

"No," said he, "it is all in vain. If someone would but tell me."

The second night he again went up into the old castle, sat down by the fire, and once more began his old song, "If I could but shudder." When midnight came, an uproar and noise of tumbling about was heard; at first it was low, but it grew louder and louder. Then it was quiet for a while, and at length with a loud scream, half a man came down the chimney and fell before him. "Hollo!" cried he. "Another half belongs to this. This is too little!" Then the uproar began again, there was a roaring and howling, and the other half fell down likewise. "Wait," said he, "I will just blow up the fire a little for thee." When he had done that and looked round again, the two pieces were joined together, and a frightful man was sitting in his place. "That is no part of our bargain," said the youth, "the bench is mine." The man wanted to push him away; the youth, however, would not allow that but thrust him off with all his strength and seated himself again in his own place.

Then still more men fell down, one after the other; they brought nine dead men's legs and two skulls, and set them up and played at nine-pins with them. The youth also wanted to play and said, "Hark you, can I join you?"

"Yes, if thou hast any money."

"Money enough," replied he, "but your balls are not quite round." Then he took the skulls and put them in the lathe and turned them till they were round. "There, now, they will roll better!" said he. "Hurrah! Now it goes merrily!" He played with them and lost some of his money, but when it struck twelve, everything vanished from his sight. He lay down and quietly fell asleep.

Next morning the king came to inquire after him. "How has it fared with you this time?" asked he.

"I have been playing at nine-pins," he answered, "and have lost a couple of farthings."

"Hast thou not shuddered then?"

"Eh, what?" said he. "I have made merry. If I did but know what it was to shudder!"

The third night he sat down again on his bench and said quite sadly, "If I could but shudder." When it grew late, six tall men came in and brought a coffin. Then said he, "Ha-ha, that is certainly my little cousin, who died only a few days ago." And he beckoned with his finger and cried, "Come, little cousin, come." They placed the coffin on the ground, but he went to it and took the lid off, and a dead man lay therein. He felt his face, but it was cold as ice. "Stop," said he. "I will warm thee a little," and went to the fire and warmed his hand and laid it on the dead man's face, but he remained cold. Then he took him out, and sat down by the fire and laid him on his breast and rubbed his arms that the blood might circulate again. As this also did no good, he thought to himself, "When two people lie in bed together, they warm each other," and carried him to the bed, covered him over, and lay down by him.

After a short time the dead man became warm, too, and began to move. Then said the youth, "See, little cousin, have I not warmed thee?"

The dead man, however, got up and cried, "Now will I strangle thee."

"What!" said he. "Is that the way thou thankest me? Thou shalt at once go into thy coffin again," and he took him up, threw him into it, and shut the lid. Then came the six men and carried him away again. "I cannot manage to shudder," said he. "I shall never learn it here as long as I live."

Then a man entered who was taller than all others, and looked terrible. He was old, however, and had a long white beard. "Thou wretch," cried he, "thou shalt soon learn what it is to shudder, for thou shalt die."

"Not so fast," replied the youth. "If I am to die, I shall have to have a say in it."

"I will soon seize thee," said the fiend.

"Softly, softly, do not talk so big. I am as strong as thou art, and perhaps even stronger."

"We shall see," said the old man. "If thou art stronger, I will let thee go—come, we will try." Then he led him by dark passages to a smith's forge, took an axe, and with one blow struck an anvil into the ground.

"I can do better than that," said the youth, and went to the other anvil. The old man placed himself near and wanted to look on, and his white beard hung down. Then the youth seized the axe, split the anvil with one blow, and struck the old man's beard in with it. "Now I have thee," said the youth. "Now it is thou who will have to die." Then he seized an iron bar and beat the old man till he moaned and entreated him to stop, and he would give him great riches. The youth drew out the axe and let him go.

The old man led him back into the castle, and in a cellar showed him three

chests full of gold. "Of these," said he, "one part is for the poor, the other for the king, the third is thine."

In the meantime it struck twelve, and the spirit disappeared; the youth, therefore, was left in darkness. "I shall still be able to find my way out," said he, and felt about, found the way into the room, and slept there by his fire.

Next morning the king came and said, "Now thou must have learnt what shuddering is."

"No," he answered; "what can it be? My dead cousin was here, and a bearded man came and showed me a great deal of money down below, but no one told me what it was to shudder."

"Then," said the king, "thou hast delivered the castle, and shalt marry my daughter."

"That is all very well," said he, "but still I do not know what it is to shudder."

Then the gold was brought up and the wedding celebrated; but howsoever much the young king loved his wife, and however happy he was, he still said always, "If I could but shudder—if I could but shudder."

And at last she was angry at this. Her waiting-maid said, "I will find a cure for him; he shall soon learn what it is to shudder." She went out to the stream which flowed through the garden, and had a whole bucketful of gudgeons brought to her.

At night when the young king was sleeping, his wife was to draw the clothes off him and empty the bucketful of cold water with the gudgeons in it over him, so that the little fishes would sprawl about him.

When this was done, he woke up and cried, "Oh, what makes me shudder so? What makes me shudder so, dear wife? Ah! now I know what it is to shudder!"

# The Wolf and the Seven Little Kids

HERE WAS ONCE UPON A TIME AN OLD GOAT WHO had seven little kids, and loved them with all the love of a mother for her children. One day she wanted to go into the forest and fetch some food. So she called all seven to her and said, "Dear children, I have to go into the forest. Be on your guard against the wolf; if he come in, he will devour you all—skin, hair, and all. The wretch often disguises himself, but you will know him at once by his rough voice and his black feet."

The kids said, "Dear mother, we will take good care of ourselves; you may go away without any anxiety." Then the old one bleated, and went on her way with an easy mind.

It was not long before someone knocked at the house-door and called, "Open the door, dear children; your mother is here and has brought something back with her for each of you."

But the little kids knew that it was the wolf by the rough voice. "We will not open the door," cried they. "Thou art not our mother. She has a soft, pleasant voice, but thy voice is rough; thou art the wolf!"

Then the wolf went away to a shopkeeper and bought himself a great lump of chalk, ate this, and made his voice soft with it. The he came back, knocked at the door of the house, and cried, "Open the door, dear children; your mother is here and has brought something back with her for each of you."

But the wolf had laid his black paws against the window, and the children saw them and cried, "We will not open the door. Our mother has not black feet like thee; thou art the wolf."

Then the wolf ran to a baker and said, "I have hurt my feet. Rub some dough over them for me." And when the baker had rubbed his feet over, he ran to the miller and said, "Strew some white meal over my feet for me."

The miller thought to himself, "The wolf wants to deceive someone," and refused.

But the wolf said, "If thou wilt not do it, I will devour thee." Then the miller was afraid, and made his paws white for him. Truly men are like that.

So now the wretch went for the third time to the house-door, knocked at it, and said, "Open the door for me, children; your dear little mother has come home and has brought every one of you something back from the forest with her."

The little kids cried, "First show us thy paws that we may know if thou art our dear little mother." Then he put his paws in through the window, and when the kids saw that they were white, they believed that all he said was true and opened the door. But who should come in but the wolf! They were terrified and wanted to hide themselves. One sprang under the table, the second into the bed, the third into the stove, the fourth into the kitchen, the fifth into the cupboard, the sixth under the washing-bowl, and the seventh into the clock-case. But the wolf found them all, and used no great ceremony; one after the other he swallowed them down his throat. The youngest, who was in the clock-case, was the only one he did not find.

When the wolf had satisfied his appetite he took himself off, laid himself down under a tree in the green meadow outside, and began to sleep.

Soon afterwards the old goat came home again from the forest. Ah! What a sight she saw there! The house-door stood wide open. The table, chairs, and benches were thrown down, the washing-bowl lay broken to pieces, and the quilts and pillows were pulled off the beds. She sought her children, but they were nowhere to be found. She called them one after another by name, but no one answered. At last, when she came to the youngest, a soft voice cried, "Dear mother, I am in the clock-case." She took the kid out, and it told her that the wolf had come and had eaten all the others. Then you may imagine how she wept over her poor children.

At length in her grief she went out, and the youngest kid ran with her. When they came to the meadow, there lay the wolf by the tree and snored so loud that the branches shook. She looked at him on every side and saw that something was moving and struggling in his gorged belly. "Ah, heavens," said she, "is it possible that my poor children, whom he has swallowed down for his supper, can be still alive?"

Then the kid had to run home and fetch scissors and a needle and thread, and the goat cut open the monster's stomach. And hardly had she made one

cut than one little kid thrust its head out; and when she cut farther, all six sprang out one after another and were all still alive and had suffered no injury whatever, for in his greediness the monster had swallowed them down whole. What rejoicing there was! They embraced their dear mother and jumped like a sailor at his wedding. The mother, however, said, "Now go and look for some big stones, and we will fill the wicked beast's stomach with them while he is still asleep."

Then the seven kids dragged the stones thither with all speed and put as many of them into his stomach as they could get in; and the mother sewed him up again in the greatest haste, so that he was not aware of anything and never once stirred.

When the wolf at length had had his sleep out, he got on his legs, and as the stones in his stomach made him very thirsty, he wanted to go to a well to drink. But when he began to walk and move about, the stones in his stomach knocked against one another and rattled. Then cried he,

*"What rumbles and tumbles*
*Against my poor bones?*
*I thought 'twas six kids,*
*But it's naught but big stones."*

And when he got to the well and stooped over the water and was just about to drink, the heavy stones made him fall in; and there was no help, but he had to drown miserably. When the seven kids saw that, they came running to the spot and cried aloud, "The wolf is dead! The wolf is dead!" and danced for joy round about the well with their mother.

# Rapunzel

HERE WERE ONCE A MAN AND A WOMAN WHO HAD long in vain wished for a child. At length the woman hoped that God was about to grant her desire. These people had a little window at the back of their house from which a splendid garden could be seen, which was full of the most beautiful flowers and herbs. It was, however, surrounded by a high wall, and no one dared to go into it because it belonged to an enchantress, who had great power and was dreaded by all the world. One day the woman was standing by this window and looking down into the garden, when she saw a bed which was planted with the most beautiful rampion, and it looked so fresh and green that she longed for it and had the greatest desire to eat some. This desire increased every day, and as she knew that she could not get any of it, she quite pined away, and looked pale and miserable. Then her husband was alarmed, and asked, "What aileth thee, dear wife?"

"Ah," she replied, "if I can't get some of the rampion, which is in the garden behind our house, to eat, I shall die."

The man, who loved her, thought, "Sooner than let thy wife die, bring her some of the rampion thyself, let it cost thee what it will." In the twilight of the evening, he clambered down over the wall into the garden of the enchantress, hastily clutched a handful of rampion, and took it to his wife. She at once made herself a salad of it and ate it with much relish. She, however, liked it so much—so very much—that the next day she longed for it three times as much as before.

If he was to have any rest, her husband must once more descend into the garden. In the gloom of evening, therefore, he let himself down again; but when he had clambered down the wall, he was terribly afraid, for he saw the enchantress standing before him. "How canst thou dare," said she with an angry look, "to descend into my garden and steal my rampion like a thief? Thou shalt suffer for it!"

"Ah," answered he, "let mercy take the place of justice. I only made up my mind to do it out of necessity. My wife saw your rampion from the window, and felt such a longing for it that she would have died if she had not got some to eat."

Then the enchantress allowed her anger to be softened, and said to him, "If the case be as thou sayest, I will allow thee to take away with thee as much rampion as thou wilt, only I make one condition: thou must give me the child which thy wife will bring into the world. It shall be well treated, and I will care for it like a mother." The man in his terror consented to everything; and when the woman was brought to bed, the enchantress appeared at once, gave the

child the name of Rapunzel, and took it away with her.

Rapunzel grew into the most beautiful child beneath the sun. When she was twelve years old, the enchantress shut her into a tower, which lay in a forest and had neither stairs nor door, but quite at the top was a little window. When the enchantress wanted to go in, she placed herself beneath it and cried,

*"Rapunzel, Rapunzel,*
*Let down thy hair to me."*

Rapunzel had magnificent long hair, fine as spun gold; and when she heard the voice of the enchantress, she unfastened her braided tresses, wound them round one of the hooks of the window above, and then the hair fell twenty ells down, and the enchantress climbed up by it.

After a year or two, it came to pass that the king's son rode through the forest and went by the tower. Then he heard a song, which was so charming that he stood still and listened. This was Rapunzel, who in her solitude passed her time in letting her sweet voice resound. The king's son wanted to climb up to her, and looked for the door of the tower, but none was to be found. He rode home, but the singing had so deeply touched his heart that every day he went out into the forest and listened to it. Once when he was thus standing behind a tree, he saw that an enchantress came there, and he heard how she cried,

*"Rapunzel, Rapunzel,*
*Let down thy hair."*

Then Rapunzel let down the braids of her hair, and the enchantress climbed up to her. "If that is the ladder by which one mounts, I will for once try my fortune," said he, and the next day when it began to grow dark, he went to the tower and cried,

*"Rapunzel, Rapunzel,*
*Let down thy hair."*

Immediately the hair fell down and the king's son climbed up. At first Rapunzel was terribly frightened when a man such as her eyes had never yet beheld came to her; but the king's son began to talk to her quite like a friend, and told her that his heart had been so stirred that it had let him have no rest, and he had been forced to see her.

Then Rapunzel lost her fear; and when he asked her if she would take him for her husband, and she saw that he was young and handsome, she thought, "He will love me more than old Dame Gothel does"; and she said yes and laid her hand in his. She said, "I will willingly go away with thee, but I do not know how to get down. Bring with thee a skein of silk every time that thou comest, and I will weave a ladder with it, and when that is ready I will descend, and thou wilt take me on thy horse."

They agreed that until that time he should come to her every evening, for the old woman came by day. The enchantress remarked nothing of this, until once Rapunzel said to her, "Tell me, Dame Gothel, how it happens that you are so much heavier for me to draw up than the young king's son—he is with me in a moment."

"Ah, thou wicked child!" cried the enchantress. "What do I hear thee say? I thought I had separated thee from all the world, and yet thou hast deceived me." In her anger she clutched Rapunzel's beautiful tresses, wrapped them twice round her left hand, seized a pair of scissors with the right, and, snip, snap, they were cut off, and the lovely braids lay on the ground. And she was so pitiless that she took poor Rapunzel into a desert where she had to live in great grief and misery.

On the same day, however, that she cast out Rapunzel, the enchantress in the evening fastened the braids of hair, which she had cut off, to the hook of the window, and when the king's son came and cried,

*"Rapunzel, Rapunzel,*
*Let down thy hair,"*

she let the hair down. The king's son ascended, but he did not find his dearest Rapunzel above but the enchantress, who gazed at him with wicked and venomous looks.

"Aha!" she cried mockingly. "Thou wouldst fetch thy dearest, but the beautiful bird sits no longer singing in the nest; the cat has got it and will scratch out thy eyes as well. Rapunzel is lost to thee; thou wilt never see her more."

The king's son was beside himself with pain, and in his despair he leapt down from the

tower. He escaped with his life, but the thorns, into which he fell, pierced his eyes. Then he wandered quite blind about the forest, ate nothing but roots and berries, and did nothing but lament and weep over the loss of his dearest wife. Thus he roamed about in misery for some years, and at length came to the desert where Rapunzel, with the twins to which she had given birth, a boy and a girl, lived in wretchedness. He heard a voice, and it seemed so familiar to him that he went towards it, and when he approached, Rapunzel knew him and fell on his neck and wept. Two of her tears wetted his eyes and they grew clear again, and he could see with them as before. He led her to his kingdom, where he was joyfully received, and they lived for a long time afterwards, happy and contented.

# The Wonderful Musician

HERE WAS ONCE A WONDERFUL MUSICIAN, WHO went quite alone through a forest and thought of all manner of things; and when nothing was left for him to think about, he said to himself, "Time is beginning to pass heavily with me here in the forest. I will fetch hither a good companion for myself." Then he took his fiddle from his back and played so that it echoed through the trees. It was not long before a wolf came trotting through the thicket towards him. "Ah, here is a wolf coming! I have no desire for him!" said the musician.

But the wolf came nearer and said to him, "Ah, dear musician, how beautifully thou dost play. I should like to learn that, too."

"It is soon learnt," the musician replied. "Thou hast only to do all that I bid thee."

"Oh, musician," said the wolf, "I will obey thee as a scholar obeys his master."

The musician bade him follow, and when they had gone part of the way together, they came to an old oak tree which was hollow inside and cleft in the middle. "Look," said the musician, "if thou wilt learn to fiddle, put thy forepaws into this crevice." The wolf obeyed, but the musician quickly picked up a stone and with one blow wedged his two paws so fast that he was forced to stay there like a prisoner. "Stay there until I come back again," said the musician, and went his way.

After a while he again said to himself, "Time is beginning to pass heavily with me here in the forest; I will fetch hither another companion," and took his fiddle and again played in the forest. It was not long before a fox came creeping through the trees towards him. "Ah, there's a fox coming!" said the musician. "I have no desire for him."

The fox came up to him and said, "Oh, dear musician, how beautifully thou dost play! I should like to learn that, too."

"That is soon learnt," said the musician. "Thou hast only to do everything that I bid thee."

"Oh, musician," then said the fox, "I will obey thee as a scholar obeys his master."

"Follow me," said the musician; and when they had walked a part of the way, they came to a footpath with high bushes on both sides of it. There the musician stood still, and from one side bent a young hazel bush down to the ground and put his foot on the top of it; then he bent down a young tree from the other side as well, and said, "Now little fox, if thou wilt learn something, give me thy left front paw." The fox obeyed, and the musician fastened his paw to the left bough. "Little fox," said he, "now reach me thy right paw" and he tied it to the right bough. When he had examined whether they were firm enough, he let go, and the bushes sprang up again, and jerked up the little fox, so that it hung struggling in the air. "Wait there till I come back again," said the musician, and went on his way.

Again he said to himself, "Time is beginning to pass heavily with me here in the forest; I will fetch hither another companion," so he took his fiddle, and the sound echoed through the forest. Then a little hare came springing towards him. "Why, a hare is coming," said the musician. "I do not want him."

"Ah, dear musician," said the hare, "how beautifully thou dost fiddle; I, too, should like to learn that."

"That is soon learnt," said the musician. "Thou hast only to do everything that I bid thee."

"Oh, musician," replied the little hare, "I will obey thee as a scholar obeys his master."

They went part of the way together until they came to an open space in the forest, where stood an aspen tree. The musician tied a long string round the little hare's neck, the other end of which he fastened to the tree. "Now briskly, little hare, run twenty times round the tree!" cried the musician, and the little hare obeyed. And when it had run round twenty times, it had twisted the string twenty times round the trunk of the tree, and the little hare was caught; and let it pull and tug as it liked, it only made the string cut into its tender neck. "Wait there till I come back," said the musician, and went onwards.

The wolf, in the meantime, had pushed and pulled and bitten at the stone, and had worked so long that he had set his feet at liberty and had drawn them

once more out of the cleft. Full of anger and rage he hurried after the musician and wanted to tear him to pieces. When the fox saw him running, he began to lament and cried with all his might, "Brother wolf, come to my help, the musician has betrayed me!" The wolf drew down the little tree, bit the cord in two, and freed the fox, who went with him to take revenge on the musician. They found the tied-up hare, whom likewise they delivered, and then they all sought the enemy together.

The musician had once more played his fiddle as he went on his way, and this time he had been more fortunate. The sound reached the ears of a poor wood-cutter, who instantly, whether he would or no, gave up his work and came with his hatchet under his arm to listen to the music. "At last comes the right companion," said the musician, "for I was seeking a human being and no wild beast." And he began and played so beautifully and delightfully that the poor man stood there as if bewitched, and his heart leapt with gladness.

And as he thus stood, the wolf, the fox, and the hare came up, and he saw well that they had some evil design. So he raised his glittering axe and placed himself before the musician, as if to say, "Whoso wishes to touch him, let him beware, for he will have to do with me!" Then the beasts were terrified and ran back into the forest. The musician, however, played once more to the man out of gratitude, and then went onwards.

# The Twelve Brothers

HERE WERE ONCE ON A TIME A KING AND A QUEEN who lived happily together and had twelve children, but they were all boys. Then said the king to his wife, "If the thirteenth child, which thou art about to bring into the world, is a girl, the twelve boys shall die in order that her possessions may be great and that the kingdom may fall to her alone." He caused likewise twelve coffins to be made, which were already filled with shavings, and in each lay the little pillow for the dead, and he had them taken into a locked-up room, and then he gave the queen the key of it and bade her not to speak of this to anyone.

The mother, however, now sat and lamented all day long, until the youngest son, who was always with her, and whom she had named Benjamin from the Bible, said to her, "Dear mother, why art thou so sad?"

"Dearest child," she answered, "I may not tell thee." But he let her have no rest until she went and unlocked the room and showed him the twelve coffins ready filled with shavings. Then she said, "My dearest Benjamin, thy father has had these coffins made for thee and for thy eleven brothers; for if I bring a little girl into the world, you are all to be killed and buried in them."

And as she wept while she was saying this, the son comforted her and said, "Weep not, dear mother, we will save ourselves and go hence."

But she said, "Go forth into the forest with thy eleven brothers, and let one sit constantly on the highest tree which can be found and keep watch, looking towards the tower here in the castle. If I give birth to a little son, I will put up a white flag, and then you may venture to come back, but if I bear a daughter, I will hoist a red flag, and then fly hence as quickly as you are able, and may the good God protect you. And every night I will rise up and pray for you—in winter that you may be able to warm yourself at a fire, and in summer that you may not faint away in the heat."

After she had blessed her sons therefore, they went forth into the forest. They each kept watch in turn, and sat on the highest oak and looked towards

the tower. When eleven days had passed and the turn came to Benjamin, he saw that a flag was being raised. It was, however, not the white, but the blood-red flag which announced that they were all to die. When the brothers heard that, they were very angry and said, "Are we all to suffer death for the sake of a girl? We swear that we will avenge ourselves! Wheresoever we find a girl, her red blood shall flow."

Thereupon they went deeper into the forest; and in the midst of it, where it was the darkest, they found a little bewitched hut, which was standing empty. Then said they, "Here we will dwell, and thou, Benjamin, who art the youngest and weakest, thou shalt stay at home and keep house; we others will go out and get food." Then they went into the forest and shot hares, wild deer, birds, and pigeons, and whatsoever there was to eat; this they took to Benjamin, who had to dress it for them in order that they might appease their hunger. They lived together ten years in the little hut, and the time did not appear long to them.

The little daughter, which their mother the queen had given birth to, was now grown-up; she was good of heart and fair of face and had a golden star on her forehead. Once, when it was the great washing, she saw twelve men's shirts among the things, and asked her mother, "To whom do these twelve shirts belong, for they are far too small for Father?"

Then the queen answered with a heavy heart, "Dear child, these belong to thy twelve brothers."

Said the maiden, "Where are my twelve brothers? I have never yet heard of them."

She replied, "God knows where they are; they are wandering about the world." Then she took the maiden and opened the chamber for her, and showed her the twelve coffins with the shavings and pillows for the heads. "These coffins," said she, "were destined for thy brothers, but they went away secretly before thou wert born," and she related to her how everything had happened.

Then said the maiden, "Dear mother, weep not. I will go and seek my brothers."

So she took the twelve shirts and went forth, and straight into the great forest. She walked the whole day, and in the evening she came to the bewitched hut. Then she entered it and found a young boy, who asked, "From whence comest thou, and whither art thou bound?" and was astonished that she was so beautiful and wore royal garments and had a star on her forehead.

And she answered, "I am a king's daughter, and am seeking my twelve brothers; and I will walk as far as the sky is blue until I find them." She likewise showed him the twelve shirts which belonged to them.

Then Benjamin saw that she was his sister, and said, "I am Benjamin, thy youngest brother." And she began to weep for joy, and Benjamin wept also, and they kissed and embraced each other with the greatest love. But after this he said, "Dear sister, there is still one difficulty. We have agreed that every maiden whom we meet shall die, because we have been obliged to leave our kingdom on account of a girl."

Then said she, "I will willingly die, if by so doing I can deliver my twelve brothers."

"No," answered he, "thou shalt not die; seat thyself beneath this tub until our eleven brothers come, and then I will soon come to an agreement with them."

She did so, and when it was night the others came from hunting, and their dinner was ready. And as they were sitting at table and eating, they asked, "What news is there?"

Said Benjamin, "Don't you know anything?"

"No," they answered.

He continued, "You have been in the forest and I have stayed at home, and yet I know more than you do."

"Tell us then," they cried.

He answered, "But promise me that the first maiden who meets us shall not be killed."

"Yes," they all cried, "she shall have mercy, only do tell us."

Then said he, "Our sister is here," and he lifted up the tub, and the king's daughter came forth in her royal garments with the golden star on her forehead; and she was beautiful, delicate, and fair. Then they were all rejoiced and fell on her neck and kissed and loved her with all their hearts.

Now she stayed at home with Benjamin and helped him with the work. The eleven went into the forest and caught game and deer and birds and wood pigeons that they might have food, and the little sister and Benjamin took care to make it ready for them. She sought for the wood for cooking and herbs for vegetables, and put the pans on the fire so that the dinner was always ready when the eleven came. She likewise kept order in the little house, and put beautifully white clean coverings on the little beds, and the brothers were always contented and lived in great harmony with her.

Once on a time the two at home had prepared a beautiful entertainment, and when they were all together, they sat down and ate and drank and were full of gladness. There was, however, a little garden belonging to the bewitched house wherein stood twelve lily flowers, which are likewise called students.

She wished to give her brothers pleasure, and plucked the twelve flowers, and thought she would present each brother with one while at dinner. But at the selfsame moment that she plucked the flowers, the twelve brothers were changed into twelve ravens and flew away over the forest, and the house and garden vanished likewise. And now the poor maiden was alone in the wild forest; and when she looked around, an old woman was standing near her who said, "My child, what hast thou done? Why didst thou not leave the twelve white flowers growing? They were thy brothers, who are now forevermore changed into ravens."

The maiden said, weeping, "Is there no way of delivering them?"

"No," said the woman, "there is but one in the whole world, and that is so hard that thou wilt not deliver them by it: for thou must be dumb for seven years and mayest not speak or laugh, and if thou speakest one single word, and only an hour of the seven years is wanting, all is in vain, and thy brothers will be killed by the one word."

Then said the maiden in her heart, "I know with certainty that I shall set my brothers free," and went and sought a high tree and seated herself in it and span, and neither spoke nor laughed.

Now it so happened that a king was hunting in the forest, who had a great greyhound which ran to the tree on which the maiden was sitting, and sprang about it, whining and barking at her. Then the king came by and saw the beautiful king's daughter with the golden star on her brow, and was so charmed with her beauty that he called to ask her if she would be his wife. She made no answer but nodded a little with her head. So he climbed up the tree himself, carried her down, placed her on his horse, and bore her home. Then the wedding was solemnized with great magnificence and rejoicing, but the

bride neither spoke nor smiled.

When they had lived happily together for a few years, the king's mother, who was a wicked woman, began to slander the young queen, and said to the king, "This is a common beggar girl whom thou hast brought back with thee. Who knows what impious tricks she practices secretly! Even if she be dumb, and not able to speak, she still might laugh for once; but those who do not laugh have bad consciences." At first the king would not believe it, but the old woman urged this so long, and accused her of so many evil things, that at last the king let himself be persuaded and sentenced her to death.

And now a great fire was lighted in the courtyard in which she was to be burnt, and the king stood above at the window and looked on with tearful eyes, because he still loved her so much. And when she was bound fast to the stake, and the fire was licking at her clothes with its red tongue, the last instant of the seven years expired. Then a whirring sound was heard in the air, and twelve ravens came flying towards the place, and sank downwards; and when they touched the earth they were her twelve brothers, whom she had delivered. They tore the fire asunder, extinguished the flames, set their dear sister free, and kissed and embraced her. And now as she dared to open her mouth and speak, she told the king why she had been dumb and had never laughed. The king rejoiced when he heard that she was innocent, and they all lived in great unity until their death. The wicked mother was taken before the judge, and put into a barrel filled with boiling oil and venomous snakes, and died an evil death.

# The Pack of Ragamuffins

THE COCK ONCE SAID TO THE HEN, "IT IS NOW THE time when our nuts are ripe, so let us go to the hill together and for once eat our fill before the squirrel takes them all away."

"Yes," replied the hen. "Come, we will have some pleasure together." Then they went away to the hill, and as it was a bright day they stayed till evening. Now I do not know whether it was that they had eaten till they were too fat, or whether they had become proud, but they would not go home on foot, and the cock had to build a little carriage of nutshells. When it was ready, the little hen seated herself in it and said to the cock, "Thou canst just harness thyself to it."

"I like that!" said the cock. "I would rather go home on foot than let myself be harnessed to it; no, that is not our bargain. I do not mind being coachman and sitting on the box, but drag it myself I will not."

As they were thus disputing, a duck quacked to them, "You thieving folks, who bade you go to my nut-hill? Well, you shall suffer for it!" And she ran with open beak at the cock. But the cock also was not idle and fell boldly on the duck, and at last wounded her so with his spurs that she also begged for mercy and willingly let herself be harnessed to the carriage as a punishment.

The little cock now seated himself on the box and was coachman, and thereupon they went off in a gallop, with "Duck, go as fast as thou canst."

When they had driven a part of the way, they met two foot passengers, a pin and a needle. They cried, "Stop! stop!" and said that it would soon be as dark as pitch, and then they could not go a step farther, and that it was so dirty

on the road, and asked if they could not get into the carriage for a while. They had been at the tailor's public-house by the gate and had stayed too long over the beer. As they were thin people, who did not take up much room, the cock let them both get in, but they had to promise him and his little hen not to step on their feet.

Late in the evening they came to an inn, and as they did not like to go farther by night, and as the duck also was not strong on her feet and fell from one side to the other, they went in. The host at first made many objections—his house was already full, besides he thought they could not be very distinguished persons—but at last, as they made pleasant speeches and told him that he should have the egg that the little hen had laid on the way and should likewise keep the duck, which laid one every day, he at length said that they might stay the night. And now they had themselves well served, and feasted and rioted.

Early in the morning, when day was breaking, and everyone was asleep, the cock awoke the hen, brought the egg, pecked it open, and they ate it together, but they threw the shell on the hearth. Then they went to the needle, which was still asleep, took it by the head and stuck it into the cushion of the landlord's chair, and put the pin in his towel; and at the last without more ado they flew away over the heath.

The duck, who liked to sleep in the open air and had stayed in the yard, heard them going away, made herself merry, and found a stream, down which she swam, which was a much quicker way of traveling than being harnessed to a carriage.

The host did not get out of bed for two hours after this. He washed himself and wanted to dry himself; then the pin went over his face and made a red streak from one ear to the other. After this he went into the kitchen and wanted to light a pipe; but when he came to the hearth, the eggshell darted into his eyes. "This morning everything attacks my head," said he, and angrily sat down on his grandfather's chair; but he quickly started up again and cried, "Woe is me," for the needle had pricked him still worse than the pin, and not in the head. Now he was thoroughly angry, and suspected the guests who had come so late the night before; and when he went and looked about for them, they were gone. Then he made a vow to take no more ragamuffins into his house, for they consume much, pay for nothing, and play mischievous tricks into the bargain by way of gratitude.

# Little Brother and Little Sister

ITTLE BROTHER TOOK HIS SISTER BY THE HAND AND said, "Since our mother died we have had no happiness. Our stepmother beats us every day; and if we come near her she kicks us away with her foot. Our meals are the hard crusts of bread that are left over; and the little dog under the table is better off, for she often throws it a nice bit. May heaven pity us. If our mother only knew! Come, we will go forth together into the wide world."

They walked the whole day over meadows, fields, and stony places; and when it rained the little sister said, "Heaven and our hearts are weeping together." In the evening they came to a large forest, and they were so weary with sorrow and hunger and the long walk that they lay down in a hollow tree and fell asleep.

The next day when they awoke, the sun was already high in the sky and shone down hot into the tree. Then the brother said, "Sister, I am thirsty; if I knew of a little brook, I would go and just take a drink; I think I hear one running." The brother got up and took the little sister by the hand, and they set off to find the brook.

But the wicked stepmother was a witch, and had seen how the two children had gone away and had crept after them privily, as witches do creep, and had bewitched all the brooks in the forest.

Now when they found a little brook leaping brightly over the stones, the brother was going to drink out of it, but the sister heard how it said as it ran, "Who drinks of me will be a tiger; who drinks of me will be a tiger."

Then the sister cried, "Pray, dear brother, do not drink, or you will become a wild beast and tear me to pieces."

The brother did not drink, although he was so thirsty, but said, "I will wait for the next spring."

When they came to the next brook, the sister heard this also say, "Who drinks of me will be a wolf; who drinks of me will be a wolf."

Then the sister cried out, "Pray, dear brother, do not drink, or you will become a wolf and devour me."

The brother did not drink, and said, "I will wait until we come to the next spring, but then I must drink, say what you like; for my thirst is too great."

And when they came to the third brook the sister heard how it said as it ran, "Who drinks of me will be a roebuck; who drinks of me will be a roebuck."

The sister said, "Oh, I pray you, dear brother, do not drink, or you will become a roebuck and run away from me." But the brother had knelt down at

once by the brook, and had bent down and drunk some of the water, and as soon as the first drops touched his lips he lay there, a young roebuck.

And now the sister wept over her poor bewitched brother, and the little roe wept also and sat sorrowfully near to her. But at last the girl said, "Be quiet, dear little roe. I will never, never leave you."

Then she untied her golden garter and put it round the roebuck's neck, and she plucked rushes and wove them into a soft cord. With this she tied the little beast and led it on, and she walked deeper and deeper into the forest.

And when they had gone a very long way they came at last to a little house, and the girl looked in; and as it was empty, she thought, "We can stay here and live." Then she sought for leaves and moss to make a soft bed for the roe; and every morning she went out and gathered roots and berries and nuts for herself and brought tender grass for the roe, who ate out of her hand and was content and played round about her. In the evening, when the sister was tired and had said her prayers, she laid her head upon the roebuck's back: that was her pillow, and she slept softly on it. And if only the brother had had his human form, it would have been a delightful life.

For some time they were alone like this in the wilderness. But it happened that the king of the country held a great hunt in the forest. Then the blasts of the horns, the barking of dogs, and the merry shouts of the huntsmen rang through the trees; and the roebuck heard all, and was only too anxious to be there. "Oh," said he to his sister, "let me be off to the hunt. I cannot bear it any longer"; and he begged so much that at last she agreed.

"But," said she to him, "come back to me in the evening; I must shut my door for fear of the rough huntsmen, so knock and say, 'My little sister, let me in!' that I may know you; and if you do not say that, I shall not open the door." Then the young roebuck sprang away; so happy was he and so merry in the open air.

The king and the huntsmen saw the pretty creature and started after him, but they could not catch him; and when they thought that they surely had him, away he sprang through the bushes and could not be seen.

When it was dark, he ran to the cottage, knocked, and said, "My little sister, let me in." Then the door was opened for him, and he jumped in and rested himself the whole night through upon his soft bed.

The next day the hunt went on afresh, and when the roebuck again heard the bugle horn and the "ho! ho!" of the huntsmen, he had no peace but said, "Sister, let me out. I must be off."

His sister opened the door for him, and said, "But you must be here again in the evening and say your password."

When the king and his huntsmen again saw the young roebuck with the golden collar, they all chased him, but he was too quick and nimble for them. This went on for the whole day, but at last by the evening the huntsmen had surrounded him, and one of them wounded him a little in the foot, so that he limped and ran slowly. Then a hunter crept after him to the cottage and heard how he said, "My little sister, let me in," and saw that the door was opened for him, and was shut again at once.

The huntsman took notice of it all, and went to the king and told him what he had seen and heard. Then the king said, "Tomorrow we will hunt once more."

The little sister, however, was dreadfully frightened when she saw that her fawn was hurt. She washed the blood off him, laid herbs on the wound, and said, "Go to your bed, dear roe, that you may get well again." But the wound was so slight that the roebuck, next morning, did not feel it anymore.

And when he again heard the sport outside, he said, "I cannot bear it, I must be there; they shall not find it so easy to catch me."

The sister cried, and said, "This time they will kill you, and here am I alone in the forest and forsaken by all the world. I will not let you out."

"Then you will have me die of grief," answered the roe. "When I hear the bugle horns, I feel as if I must jump out of my skin." Then the sister could not do otherwise but opened the door for him with a heavy heart; and the roebuck, full of health and joy, bounded into the forest.

When the king saw him, he said to his huntsmen, "Now chase him all day long till nightfall, but take care that no one does him any harm."

As soon as the sun had set, the king said to the huntsman, "Now come and show me the cottage in the wood"; and when he was at the door, he knocked and called out, "Dear little sister, let me in." Then the door opened, and the king walked in, and there stood a maiden more lovely than any he had ever seen. The maiden was frightened when she saw not her little roe but a man come in who wore a golden crown upon his head. But the king looked kindly at her, stretched out his hand, and said, "Will you go with me to my palace and be my dear wife?"

"Yes, indeed," answered the maiden, "but the little roe must go with me, I cannot leave him."

The king said, "It shall stay with you as long as you live, and shall want nothing." Just then he came running in, and the sister again tied him with the cord of rushes, took it in her own hand, and went away with the king from the cottage.

The king took the lovely maiden upon his horse and carried her to his palace, where the wedding was held with great pomp. She was now the queen, and they lived for a long time happily together; the roebuck was tended and cherished, and ran about in the palace garden.

But the wicked stepmother, because of whom the children had gone out into the world, thought all the time that the sister had been torn to pieces by the wild beasts in the wood and that the brother had been shot for a roebuck by the huntsmen. Now when she heard that they were so happy, and so well off, envy and hatred rose in her heart and left her no peace; and she thought of nothing but how she could bring them again to misfortune. Her own daughter, who was ugly as night and had only one eye, grumbled at her and said, "A queen! That ought to have been my luck."

"Only be quiet," answered the old woman, and comforted her by saying, "When the time comes, I shall be ready."

As time went on, the queen had a pretty little boy, and it happened that the king was out hunting; so the old witch took the form of the chambermaid, went into the room where the queen lay, and said to her, "Come, the bath is ready; it will do you good and give you fresh strength. Make haste before it gets cold."

The daughter also was close by; so they carried the weakly queen into the bathroom and put her into the bath; then they shut the door and ran away. But in the bathroom they had made a fire of such deadly heat that the beautiful young queen was soon suffocated.

When this was done, the old woman took her daughter, put a nightcap on her head, and laid her in bed in place of the queen. She gave her, too, the shape and the look of the queen, only she could not make good the lost eye. But in order that the king might not see it, she was to lie on the side on which she had no eye.

In the evening when he came home and heard that he had a son, he was heartily glad and was going to the bed of his dear wife to see how she was. But the old woman quickly called out, "For your life, leave the curtains closed; the queen ought not to see the light yet and must have rest." The king went away, and did not find out that a false queen was lying in the bed.

But at midnight, when all slept, the nurse, who was sitting in the nursery by the cradle and who was the only person awake, saw the door open and the true queen walk in. She took the child out of the cradle, laid it on her arm, and suckled it. Then she shook up its pillow, laid the child down again, and covered it with the little quilt. And she did not forget the roebuck but went into the corner where it lay and stroked its back. Then she went quite silently out of the door again. The next morning the

nurse asked the guards whether anyone had come into the palace during the night, but they answered, "No, we have seen no one."

She came thus many nights and never spoke a word: the nurse always saw her, but she did not dare to tell anyone about it.

When some time had passed in this manner, the queen began to speak in the night, and said—

*"How fares my child? How fares my roe?*
*Twice shall I come, then never more."*

The nurse did not answer, but when the queen had gone again, went to the king and told him all. The king said, "Ah, heavens! What is this? Tomorrow night I will watch by the child."

In the evening he went into the nursery, and at midnight the queen again appeared and said—

*"How fares my child? How fares my roe?*
*Once will I come, then never more."*

And she nursed the child as she was wont to do before she disappeared. The king dared not speak to her, but on the next night he watched again. Then she said —

*"How fares my child? How fares my roe?*
*This time I come, then never more."*

Then the king could not restrain himself; he sprang towards her, and said, "You can be none other than my dear wife."

She answered, "Yes, I am your dear wife," and at the same moment she received life again, and by God's grace became fresh, rosy, and full of health.

Then she told the king the evil deed which the wicked witch and her daughter had been guilty of towards her. The king ordered both to be led before the judge, and judgment was delivered against them. The daughter was taken into the forest, where she was torn to pieces by wild beasts, but the witch was cast into the fire and miserably burnt. And as soon as she was burnt, the roebuck changed his shape and received his human form again, so the sister and brother lived happily together all their lives.

# The Devil with the Three Golden Hairs

HERE WAS ONCE A POOR WOMAN WHO GAVE BIRTH to a little son; and as he came into the world with a caul on, it was predicted that in his fourteenth year he would have the king's daughter for his wife. It happened that soon afterwards the king came into the village, and no one knew that he was the king; and when he asked the people what news there was, they answered, "A child has just been born with a caul on; whatever anyone so born undertakes turns out well. It is prophesied, too, that in his fourteenth year he will have the king's daughter for his wife."

The king, who had a bad heart and was angry about the prophecy, went to the parents, and, seeming quite friendly, said, "You poor people, let me have your child, and I will take care of it."

At first they refused, but when the stranger offered them a large amount of gold for it, and they thought, "It is a luck-child, and everything must turn out well for it," they at last consented, and gave him the child.

The king put it in a box and rode away with it until he came to a deep piece of water; then he threw the box into it and thought, "I have freed my daughter from her unlooked-for suitor."

The box, however, did not sink, but floated like a boat, and not a drop of water made its way into it. And it floated to within two miles of the king's chief city, where there was a mill, and it came to a standstill at the mill-dam. A miller's boy, who by good luck was standing there, noticed it and pulled it out with a hook, thinking that he had found a great treasure; but when he opened it, there lay a pretty boy inside, quite fresh and lively. He took him to the miller and his wife, and as they had no children they were glad, and said, "God has given him to us." They took great care of the foundling, and he grew up in all goodness.

It happened that once in a storm, the king went into the mill, and he asked the mill folk if the tall youth was their son. "No," answered they, "he's a foundling. Fourteen years ago he floated down to the mill-dam in a box, and the mill boy pulled him out of the water."

Then the king knew that it was none other than the luck-child whom he had thrown into the water, and he said, "My good people, could not the youth take a letter to the queen? I will give him two gold pieces as a reward."

"Just as the king commands," answered they, and they told the boy to hold himself in readiness. Then the king wrote a letter to the queen, wherein he said, "As soon as the boy arrives with this letter, let him be killed and buried, and all must be done before I come home."

The boy set out with this letter; but he lost his way, and in the evening came to a large forest. In the darkness he saw a small light; he went towards it and reached a cottage. When he went in, an old woman was sitting by the fire quite alone. She started when she saw the boy, and said, "Whence do you come, and whither are you going?"

"I come from the mill," he answered, "and wish to go to the queen, to whom I am taking a letter; but as I have lost my way in the forest I should like to stay here overnight."

"You poor boy," said the woman, "you have come into a den of thieves, and when they come home, they will kill you."

"Let them come," said the boy. "I am not afraid; but I am so tired that I cannot go any farther"; and he stretched himself upon a bench and fell asleep.

Soon afterwards the robbers came, and angrily asked what strange boy was lying there. "Ah," said the old woman, "it is an innocent child who has lost himself in the forest, and out of pity I have let him come in; he has to take a letter to the queen." The robbers opened the letter and read it; and in it was written that the boy as soon as he arrived should be put to death. Then the hardhearted robbers felt pity, and their leader tore up the letter and wrote another, saying that as soon as the boy came, he should be married at once to the king's daughter. Then they let him lie quietly on the bench until the next morning, and when he awoke they gave him the letter and showed him the right way.

And the queen, when she had received the letter and read it, did as was written in it, and had a splendid wedding feast prepared, and the king's daughter was married to the luck-child, and as the youth was handsome and agreeable, she lived with him in joy and contentment.

After some time the king returned to his palace and saw that the prophecy was fulfilled and the luck-child married to his daughter. "How has that come to pass?" said he. "I gave quite another order in my letter."

So the queen gave him the letter and said that he might see for himself what was written in it. The king read the letter and saw quite well that it had been exchanged for the other. He asked the youth what had become of the letter entrusted to him, and why he had brought another instead of it. "I know nothing about it," answered he. "It must have been changed in the night, when I slept in the forest."

The king said in a passion, "You shall not have everything quite so much your own way; whosoever marries my daughter must fetch me from hell three golden hairs from the head of the devil. Bring me what I want, and you shall keep my daughter." In this way the king hoped to be rid of him forever.

But the luck-child answered, "I will fetch the golden hairs; I am not afraid of the devil." Thereupon he took leave of them and began his journey.

The road led him to a large town, where the watchman by the gates asked him what his trade was and what he knew. "I know everything," answered the luck-child.

"Then you can do us a favor," said the watchman, "if you will tell us why our market fountain, which once flowed with wine, has become dry and no longer gives even water."

"That you shall know," answered he. "Only wait until I come back."

Then he went farther and came to another town, and there also the gatekeeper asked him what was his trade and what he knew. "I know everything," answered he.

"Then you can do us a favor and tell us why a tree in our town, which once bore golden apples, now does not even put forth leaves."

"You shall know that," answered he. "Only wait until I come back."

Then he went on and came to a wide river over which he must go. The ferryman asked him what his trade was, and what he knew. "I know everything," answered he.

"Then you can do me a favor," said the ferryman, "and tell me why I must always be rowing backwards and forwards and am never set free."

"You shall know that," answered he. "Only wait until I come back."

When he had crossed the water he found the entrance to hell. It was black and sooty within, and the devil was not at home, but his grandmother was sitting in a large armchair. "What do you want?" said she to him, but she did not look so very wicked.

"I should like to have three golden hairs from the devil's head," answered he, "else I cannot keep my wife."

"That is a good deal to ask for," said she. "If the devil comes home and finds you, it will cost you your life; but as I pity you, I will see if I cannot help you."

She changed him into an ant and said, "Creep into the folds of my dress; you will be safe there."

"Yes," answered he, "so far, so good; but there are three things besides that I want to know: why a fountain which once flowed with wine has become dry and no longer gives even water; why a tree which once bore golden apples does not even put forth leaves; and why a ferryman must always be going backwards and forwards and is never set free?"

"Those are difficult questions," answered she, "but only be silent and quiet and pay attention to what the devil says when I pull out the three golden hairs."

As the evening came on, the devil returned home. No sooner had he entered than he noticed that the air was not pure. "I smell man's flesh," said he; "all is not right here." Then he pried into every corner and searched, but could not find anything.

His grandmother scolded him. "It has just been swept," said she, "and everything put in order, and now you are upsetting it again; you have always got man's flesh in your nose. Sit down and eat your supper."

When he had eaten and drunk, he was tired and laid his head in his grandmother's lap; and before long he was fast asleep, snoring and breathing heavily. Then the old woman took hold of a golden hair, pulled it out, and laid it down near her. "Oh!" cried the devil. "What are you doing?"

"I have had a bad dream," answered the grandmother, "so I seized hold of your hair."

"What did you dream then?" said the devil.

"I dreamt that a fountain in a marketplace, from which wine once flowed, was dried up and not even water would flow out of it. What is the cause of it?"

"Oh, ho! if they did but know it," answered the devil. "There is a toad sitting under a stone in the well; if they killed it, the wine would flow again."

He went to sleep again and snored until the windows shook. Then she pulled the second hair out. "Ha! What are you doing?" cried the devil angrily.

"Do not take it ill," said she. "I did it in a dream."

"What have you dreamt this time?" asked he.

"I dreamt that in a certain kingdom there stood an apple tree which had once borne golden apples but now would not even bear leaves. What, think you, was the reason?"

"Oh! if they did but know," answered the devil. "A mouse is gnawing at the root; if they killed this, they would have golden apples again, but if it gnaws much longer the tree will wither altogether. But leave me alone with your dreams: if you disturb me in my sleep again you will get a box on the ear."

The grandmother spoke gently to him until he fell asleep again and snored. Then she took hold of the third golden hair and pulled it out. The devil jumped up, roared out, and would have treated her ill if she had not quieted him once more and said, "Who can help bad dreams?"

"What was the dream, then?" asked he, and was quite curious.

"I dreamt of a ferryman who complained that he must always ferry from one side to the other and was never released. What is the cause of it?"

"Ah! the fool," answered the devil. "When anyone comes and wants to go across, he must put the oar in his hand, and the other man will have to ferry and he will be free." As the grandmother had plucked out the three golden hairs, and the three questions were answered, she let the old serpent alone,

FETCH
ME FROM
HELL
THREE GOLDEN
HAIRS
FROM THE
HEAD
OF THE DEVIL

and he slept until daybreak.

When the devil had gone out again, the old woman took the ant out of the folds of her dress and gave the luck-child his human shape again. "There are the three golden hairs for you," said she. "What the devil said to your three questions, I suppose you heard?"

"Yes," answered he, "I heard, and will take care to remember."

"You have what you want," said she, "and now you can go your way."

He thanked the old woman for helping him in his need, and left hell, well content that everything had turned out so fortunately.

When he came to the ferryman, he was expected to give the promised answer. "Ferry me across first," said the luck-child, "and then I will tell you how you can be set free," and when he reached the opposite shore he gave him the devil's advice: "Next time anyone comes who wants to be ferried over, just put the oar in his hand."

He went on and came to the town wherein stood the unfruitful tree, and there, too, the watchman wanted an answer. So he told him what he had heard from the devil: "Kill the mouse which is gnawing at its root, and it will again bear golden apples." Then the watchman thanked him and gave him as a reward two asses laden with gold, which followed him.

At last he came to the town whose well was dry. He told the watchman what the devil had said: "A toad is in the well beneath a stone; you must find it and kill it, and the well will again give wine in plenty." The watchman thanked him, and also gave him two asses laden with gold.

At last the luck-child got home to his wife, who was heartily glad to see him again, and to hear how well he had prospered in everything. To the king he took what he had asked for, the devil's three golden hairs, and when the king saw the four asses laden with gold he was quite content, and said, "Now all the conditions are fulfilled, and you can keep my daughter. But tell me, dear son-in-law, where did all that gold come from? This is tremendous wealth!"

"I was rowed across a river," answered he, "and got it there; it lies on the shore instead of sand."

"Can I, too, fetch some of it?" said the king; and he was quite eager about it.

"As much as you like," answered he. "There is a ferryman on the river; let him ferry you over, and you can fill your sacks on the other side." The greedy king set out in all haste; and when he came to the river, he beckoned to the ferryman to put him across. The ferryman came and bade him get in, and when they got to the other shore, he put the oar in his hand and sprang out. But from this time forth the king had to ferry, as a punishment for his sins. Perhaps he is ferrying still. If he is, it is because no one has taken the oar from him.

# The Three Spinning Women

HERE WAS ONCE A GIRL WHO WAS IDLE AND WOULD not spin; and let her mother say what she would, she could not bring her to it. At last the mother was once so overcome with anger and impatience that she beat her, on which the girl began to weep loudly. Now at this very moment the queen drove by; and when she heard the weeping she stopped her carriage, went into the house, and asked the mother why she was beating her daughter so that the cries could be heard out on the road. Then the woman was ashamed to reveal the laziness of her daughter and said, "I cannot get her to leave off spinning. She insists on spinning for ever and ever, and I am poor and cannot procure the flax."

Then answered the queen, "There is nothing that I like better to hear than spinning, and I am never happier than when the wheels are humming. Let me have your daughter with me in the palace. I have flax enough, and there she shall spin as much as she likes." The mother was heartily satisfied with this, and the queen took the girl with her.

When they had arrived at the palace, she led her up into three rooms which were filled from the bottom to the top with the finest flax. "Now spin me this flax," said she, "and when thou hast done it, thou shalt have my eldest son for a husband, even if thou art poor. I care not for that; thy indefatigable industry is dowry enough."

The girl was secretly terrified, for she could not have spun the flax, no, not if she had lived till she was three hundred years old and had sat at it every day from morning till night. When therefore she was alone, she began to weep, and sat thus for three days without moving a finger. On the third day came the queen, and when she saw that nothing had been spun yet, she was surprised; but the girl excused herself by saying that she had not been able to begin because of her great distress at leaving her mother's house. The queen was satisfied with this, but said when she was going away, "Tomorrow thou must begin to work."

When the girl was alone again, she did not know what to do, and in her distress went to the window. Then she saw three women coming towards her, the first of whom had a broad flat foot; the second had such a great underlip that it hung down over her chin; and the third had a broad thumb. They remained standing before the window, looked up, and asked the girl what was amiss with her. She complained of her trouble, and then they offered her their help and said, "If thou wilt invite us to the wedding, not be ashamed of us, and wilt call us thine aunts and likewise wilt place us at thy table, we will spin up the flax for thee, and that in a very short time."

"With all my heart," she replied, "do but come in and begin the work at once." Then she let in the three strange women, and cleared a place in the first room, where they seated themselves and began their spinning. The one drew the thread and trod the wheel, the other wetted the thread, the third twisted it and struck the table with her finger; and as often as she struck it, a skein of thread fell to the ground that was spun in the finest manner possible. The girl concealed the three spinners from the queen and showed her whenever she came the great quantity of spun thread, until the latter could not praise her enough.

When the first room was empty, she went to the second, and at last to the third; and that too was quickly cleared. Then the three women took leave and said to the girl, "Do not forget what thou hast promised us—it will make thy fortune."

When the maiden showed the queen the empty rooms and the great heap of yarn, she gave orders for the wedding, and the bridegroom rejoiced that he was to have such a clever and industrious wife, and praised her mightily.

"I have three aunts," said the girl, "and as they have been very kind to me, I should not like to forget them in my good fortune; allow me to invite them to the wedding and let them sit with us at table."

The queen and the bridegroom said, "Why should we not allow that?"

Therefore when the feast began, the three women entered in strange apparel, and the bride said, "Welcome, dear aunts."

"Ah," said the bridegroom, "how comest thou by these odious friends?" Thereupon he went to the one with the broad flat foot, and said, "How do you come by such a broad foot?"

"By treading," she answered, "by treading."

Then the bridegroom went to the second, and said, "How do you come by your falling lip?"

"By licking," she answered, "by licking."

Then he asked the third, "How do you come by your broad thumb?"

"By twisting the thread," she answered, "by twisting the thread."

On this the king's son was alarmed and said, "Neither now nor ever shall my beautiful bride touch a spinning-wheel." And thus she got rid of the hateful flax spinning.

# Hansel and Gretel

ARD BY A GREAT FOREST DWELT A POOR WOOD-cutter with his wife and his two children. The boy was called Hansel and the girl Gretel. He had little to bite and to break; and once when great scarcity fell on the land, he could no longer procure daily bread. Now when he thought over this by night in his bed, and tossed about in his anxiety, he groaned and said to his wife, "What is to become of us? How are we to feed our poor children, when we no longer have anything even for ourselves?"

"I'll tell you what, Husband," answered the woman. "Early tomorrow morning we will take the children out into the forest to where it is the thickest. There we will light a fire for them and give each of them one piece of bread more; and then we will go to our work and leave them alone. They will not find the way home again, and we shall be rid of them."

"No, Wife," said the man, "I will not do that. How can I bear to leave my children alone in the forest? The wild animals would soon come and tear them to pieces."

"O, thou fool!" said she. "Then we must all four die of hunger—thou mayest as well plane the planks for our coffins," and she left him no peace until he consented.

"But I feel very sorry for the poor children, all the same," said the man.

The two children had also not been able to sleep for hunger, and had heard what their stepmother had said to their father. Gretel wept bitter tears and said to Hansel, "Now all is over with us."

"Be quiet, Gretel," said Hansel. "Do not distress thyself. I will soon find a way to help us." And when the old folks had fallen asleep, he got up, put on his little coat, opened the door below, and crept outside. The moon shone brightly, and the white pebbles which lay in front of the house glittered like real silver pennies. Hansel stooped and put as many of them in the little pocket of his coat as he could possibly get in. Then he went back and said to Gretel, "Be comforted, dear little sister, and sleep in peace; God will not forsake us," and he lay down again in his bed.

When day dawned, but before the sun had risen, the woman came and awoke the two children, saying "Get up, you sluggards! We are going into the forest to fetch wood." She gave each a little piece of bread, and said, "There is something for your dinner, but do not eat it up before then, for you will get nothing else." Gretel took the bread under her apron, as Hansel had the stones in his pocket. Then they all set out together on the way to the forest. When they had walked a short time, Hansel stood still and peeped back at the house, and did so again and again.

His father said, "Hansel, what art thou looking at there and staying behind for? Mind what thou art about, and do not forget how to use thy legs."

"Ah, Father," said Hansel, "I am looking at my little white cat, which is sitting up on the roof and wants to say good-bye to me."

The wife said, "Fool, that is not thy little cat; that is the morning sun which is shining on the chimneys." Hansel, however, had not been looking back at the cat, but had been constantly throwing one of the white pebble stones out of his pocket on the road.

When they had reached the middle of the forest, the father said, "Now, children, pile up some wood, and I will light a fire that you may not be cold." Hansel and Gretel gathered brushwood together, as high as a little hill.

The brushwood was lighted; and when the flames were burning very high, the woman said, "Now, children, lay yourselves down by the fire and rest; we will go into the forest and cut some wood. When we have done, we will come back and fetch you away."

Hansel and Gretel sat by the fire, and when noon came, each ate a little piece of bread; and, as they heard the strokes of the wood-axe, they believed that their father was near. It was not, however, the axe. It was a branch which he had fastened to a withered tree that the wind was blowing backwards and forwards. And as they had been sitting such a long time, their eyes shut with fatigue, and they fell fast asleep.

When at last they awoke, it was already dark night. Gretel began to cry and said, "How are we to get out of the forest now?"

But Hansel comforted her and said, "Just wait a little, until the moon has risen, and then we will soon find the way." And when the full moon had risen, Hansel took his little sister by the hand, and followed the pebbles which shone like newly coined silver pieces, and showed them the way.

They walked the whole night long, and by break of day came once more to their father's house. They knocked at the door, and when the woman opened it and saw that it was Hansel and Gretel, she said, "You naughty children, why have you slept so long in the forest? We thought you were never coming back at all!" The father, however, rejoiced, for it had cut him to the heart to leave them behind alone.

Not long afterwards, there was once more great scarcity in all parts, and the children heard their mother saying at night to their father, "Everything is eaten again; we have one half loaf left, and after that there is an end. The children must go. We will take them farther into the wood, so that they will not find their way out again; there is no other means of saving ourselves!"

The man's heart was heavy, and he thought, "It would be better for thee to share the last mouthful with thy children." The woman, however, would listen to nothing that he had to say but scolded and reproached him. He who says A must say B, likewise; and as he had yielded the first time, he had to do so a second time also.

The children were, however, still awake and had heard the conversation. When the old folks were asleep, Hansel again got up and wanted to go out and pick up pebbles as he had done before; but the woman had locked the door, and Hansel could not get out. Nevertheless he comforted his little sister, and said, "Do not cry, Gretel. Go to sleep quietly. The good God will help us."

Early in the morning came the woman, and took the children out of their beds. Their bit of bread was given to them, but it was still smaller than the time before. On the way into the forest Hansel crumbled his in his pocket, and often stood still and threw a morsel on the ground.

"Hansel, why dost thou stop and look round?" said the father. "Go on."

"I am looking back at my little pigeon which is sitting on the roof and wants to say good-bye to me," answered Hansel.

"Simpleton!" said the woman. "That is not thy little pigeon; that is the morning sun that is shining on the chimney." Hansel, however, little by little, threw all the crumbs on the path.

The woman led the children still deeper into the forest, where they had never in their lives been before. Then a great fire was again made, and the mother said, "Just sit there, you children, and when you are tired you may sleep a little; we are going into the forest to cut wood, and in the evening when we are done, we will come and fetch you away." When it was noon, Gretel shared her piece of bread with Hansel, who had scattered his by the way. Then they fell asleep and evening came and went, but no one came to the poor children. They did not awake until it was dark night, and Hansel comforted his little sister and said, "Just wait, Gretel, until the moon rises, and then we shall see the crumbs of bread which I have strewn about. They will show us our way home again." When the moon came, they set out, but they found no crumbs, for the many thousands of birds which fly about in the woods and fields had picked them all up. Hansel said to Gretel, "We shall soon find the way," but they did not find it. They walked the whole night and all the next day, too, from morning till evening, but they did not get out of the forest and were very hungry, for they had nothing to eat but two or three berries, which grew on the ground. And as they were so weary that their legs would carry them no longer, they lay down beneath a tree and fell asleep.

It was now three mornings since they had left their father's house. They began to walk again, but they always got deeper into the forest, and if help did not come soon, they must die of hunger and weariness. When it was midday, they saw a beautiful snow-white bird sitting on a bough, which sang so delightfully that they stood still and listened to it. And when it had finished its song, it spread its wings and flew away before them, and they followed it until they reached a little house, on the roof of which it alighted; and when they came quite up to little house they saw that it was built of bread and covered with cakes but that the windows were of clear sugar. "We will set to work on that," said Hansel, "and have a good meal. I will eat a bit of the roof, and thou, Gretel, canst eat some of the window; it will taste sweet." Hansel reached up above, and broke off a little of the roof to try how it tasted, and Gretel leant against the window and nibbled at the panes. Then a soft voice cried from the room,

*"Nibble, nibble, gnaw,*
*Who is nibbling at my little house?"*

The children answered,

*"The wind, the wind,*

*The heaven-born wind,"*

and went on eating without disturbing themselves. Hansel, who thought the roof tasted very nice, tore down a great piece of it, and Gretel pushed out the whole of one round windowpane, sat down, and enjoyed herself with it.

Suddenly the door opened, and a very, very old woman, who supported herself on crutches, came creeping out. Hansel and Gretel were so terribly frightened that they let fall what they had in their hands. The old woman, however, nodded her head, and said, "Oh, you dear children, who has brought you here? Do come in, and stay with me. No harm shall happen to you." She took them both by the hand and led them into her little house. Then good food was set before them: milk and pancakes with sugar, apples, and nuts. Afterwards two pretty little beds were covered with clean white linen, and Hansel and Gretel lay down in them, and thought they were in heaven.

The old woman had only pretended to be so kind; she was in reality a wicked witch, who lay in wait for children and had only built the little house of bread in order to entice them there. When a child fell into her power, she killed it, cooked, and ate it, and that was a feast day with her. Witches have red eyes and cannot see far, but they have a keen scent like the beasts and are aware when human beings draw near. When Hansel and Gretel came into her neighborhood, she laughed maliciously and said mockingly, "I have them; they shall not escape me again!" Early in the morning before the children were awake, she was already up, and when she saw both of them sleeping and looking so pretty, with their plump red cheeks, she muttered to herself,

"That will be a dainty mouthful!" Then she seized Hansel with her shriveled hand, carried him into a little stable, and shut him in with a grated door. He might scream as he liked, that was of no use. Then she went to Gretel, shook her till she awoke, and cried, "Get up, lazy thing, fetch some water, and cook something good for thy brother. He is in the stable outside and is to be made fat. When he is fat, I will eat him." Gretel began to weep bitterly, but it was all in vain; she was forced to do what the wicked witch ordered her.

And now the best food was cooked for poor Hansel, but Gretel got nothing but crab shells. Every morning the woman crept to the little stable, and cried, "Hansel, stretch out thy finger that I may feel if thou wilt soon be fat." Hansel, however, stretched out a little bone to her, and the old woman, who had dim eyes, could not see it and thought it was Hansel's finger and was astonished that there was no way of fattening him.

When four weeks had gone by, and Hansel still continued thin, she was seized with impatience and would not wait any longer. "Hey, Gretel," she cried to the girl, "be active, and bring some water. Let Hansel be fat or lean, tomorrow I will kill him and cook him."

Ah, how the poor little sister did lament when she had to fetch the water, and how her tears did flow down over her cheeks! "Dear God, do help us," she cried. "If the wild beasts in the forest had but devoured us, we should at any rate have died together."

"Just keep thy noise to thyself," said the old woman. "All that won't help thee at all."

Early in the morning, Gretel had to go out and hang up the cauldron with the water, and light the fire. "We will bake first," said the old woman. "I have already heated the oven and kneaded the dough." She pushed poor Gretel out to the oven, from which flames of fire were already darting. "Creep in," said the witch, "and see if it is properly heated, so that we can shut the bread in." And when once Gretel was inside, she intended to shut the oven and let her bake in it, and then she would eat her, too.

But Gretel saw what she had in her mind, and said, "I do not know how I am to do it. How do you get in?"

"Silly goose," said the old woman. "The door is big enough; just look, I can get in myself!" And she crept up and thrust her head into the oven. Then Gretel gave her a push that drove her far into it, and she shut the iron door and fastened the bolt. Oh! then the witch began to howl quite horribly; but Gretel ran away, and the godless witch was miserably burnt to death.

Gretel, however, ran like lightning to Hansel, opened his little stable, and cried, "Hansel, we are saved! The old witch is dead!" Then Hansel sprang out like a bird from its cage when the door is opened for it. How they did rejoice and embrace each other, and dance about and kiss each other!

And as they had no longer any need to fear her, they went into the witch's house, and in every corner there stood chests full of pearls and jewels. "These are far better than pebbles!" said Hansel, and thrust into his pockets whatever could be got in.

And Gretel said, "I, too, will take something home with me," and filled her pinafore full.

"But now we will go away," said Hansel, "that we may get out of the witch's forest."

When they had walked for two hours, they came to a great piece of water. "We cannot get over," said Hansel. "I see no foot-plank and no bridge."

"And no boat crosses either," answered Gretel, "but a white duck is

swimming there; if I ask her, she will help us over." Then she cried,

*"Little duck, little duck, dost thou see,*
*Hansel and Gretel are waiting for thee?*
*There's never a plank or bridge in sight,*
*Take us across on thy back so white."*

The duck came to them, and Hansel seated himself on its back, and told his sister to sit by him. "No," replied Gretel, "that will be too heavy for the little duck; she shall take us across one after the other."

The good little duck did so, and when they were once safely across and had walked for a short time, the forest seemed to be more and more familiar to them; and at length they saw from afar their father's house. Then they began to run, rushed into the parlor, and threw themselves into their father's arms. The man had not known one happy hour since he had left the children in the forest; the woman, however, was dead. Gretel emptied her pinafore until pearls and precious stones ran about the room, and Hansel threw one handful after another out of his pocket to add to them. Then all anxiety was at an end, and they lived together in perfect happiness. My tale is done; there runs a mouse, whosoever catches it may make himself a big fur cap out of it.

# The Three Snake Leaves

HERE WAS ONCE ON A TIME A POOR MAN, WHO COULD no longer support his only son. Then said the son, "Dear father, things go so badly with us that I am a burden to you. I would rather go away and see how I can earn my bread." So the father gave him his blessing and with great sorrow took leave of him. At this time the king of a mighty empire was at war, and the youth took service with him, and with him went out to fight. And when he came before the enemy, there was a battle and great danger, and it rained shot until his comrades fell on all sides; and when the leader also was killed, those left were about to take flight, but the youth stepped forth, spoke boldly to them, and cried, "We will not let our fatherland be ruined!" Then the others followed him, and he pressed on and conquered the enemy. When the king heard that he owed the victory to him alone, he raised him above all the others, gave him great treasures, and made him the first in the kingdom.

The king had a daughter who was very beautiful, but she was also very strange. She had made a vow to take no one as her lord and husband who did not promise to let himself be buried alive with her if she died first. "If he loves me with all his heart," said she, "of what use will life be to him afterwards?" On her side she would do the same, and if he died first, would go down to the grave with him. This strange oath had up to this time frightened away all wooers, but the youth became so charmed with her beauty that he cared for nothing but asked her father for her.

"But dost thou know what thou must promise?" said the king.

"I must be buried with her," he replied, "if I outlive her, but my love is so great that I do not mind the danger." Then the king consented, and the wedding was solemnized with great splendor.

They lived now for a while, happy and contented with each other; and then it befell that the young queen was attacked by a severe illness, and no physician could save her. And as she lay there dead, the young king remembered what he had been obliged to promise and was horrified at having to lie down alive in the grave, but there was no escape. The king had placed sentries at all the gates, and it was not possible to avoid his fate. When the day came when the corpse was to be buried, he was taken down into the royal vault with it and then the door was shut and bolted.

Near the coffin stood a table on which were four candles, four loaves of bread, and four bottles of wine, and when this provision came to an end, he would have to die of hunger. And now he sat there, full of pain and grief, ate every day only a little piece of bread, drank only a mouthful of wine, and nevertheless saw death daily drawing nearer. Whilst he thus gazed before him, he saw a snake creep out of a corner of the vault and approach the dead body. And as he thought it came to gnaw at it, he drew his sword and said, "As long as I live, thou shalt not touch her," and hewed the snake in three pieces. After a time a second snake crept out of the hole, and when it saw the other lying dead and cut in pieces, it went back, but soon came again with three green leaves in its mouth. Then it took the three pieces of the snake, laid them together, as they ought to go, and placed one of the leaves on each wound. Immediately the severed parts joined themselves together, the snake moved and became

alive again, and both of them hastened away together. The leaves were left lying on the ground, and a desire came into the mind of the unhappy man who had been watching all this, to know if the wondrous power of the leaves that had brought the snake to life again could not likewise be of service to a human being. So he picked up the leaves and laid one of them on the mouth of his dead wife, and the two others on her eyes. And hardly had he done this than the blood stirred in her veins, rose into her pale face, and colored it again. Then she drew breath, opened her eyes, and said, "Ah, God, where am I?"

"Thou art with me, dear wife," he answered, and told her how everything had happened, and how he had brought her back again to life. Then he gave her some wine and bread, and when she had regained her strength, he raised her up and they went to the door and knocked, and called so loudly that the sentries heard it, and told the king. The king came down himself and opened the door, and there he found both strong and well, and rejoiced with them that now all sorrow was over. The young king, however, took the three snake leaves with him, gave them to a servant, and said, "Keep them for me carefully, and carry them constantly about thee; who knows in what trouble they may yet be of service to us!"

A change had, however, taken place in his wife: after she had been restored to life, it seemed as if all love for her husband had gone out of her heart. After some time, when he wanted to make a voyage over the sea, to visit his old father, and they had gone on board a ship, she forgot the great love and fidelity which he had shown her and which had been the means of rescuing her from death, and conceived a wicked inclination for the skipper. And once when the young king lay there asleep, she called in the skipper and seized the sleeper by the head, and the skipper took him by the feet, and thus they threw him down into the sea. When the shameful deed was done, she said, "Now let us return home, and say that he died on the way. I will extol and praise thee so to my father that he will marry me to thee, and make thee the heir to his crown." But the faithful servant who had seen all that they did, unseen by them, unfastened a little boat from the ship, got into it, sailed after his master, and let the traitors go on their way. He fished up the dead body, and by the help of the three snake leaves which he carried about with him, and laid on the eyes and mouth, he fortunately brought the young king back to life.

They both rowed with all their strength day and night, and their little boat flew so swiftly that they reached the old king before the others did. He was astonished when he saw them come alone and asked what had happened to them. When he learnt the wickedness of his daughter, he said, "I cannot believe that she has behaved so ill, but the truth will soon come to light," and bade both go into a secret chamber and keep themselves hidden from everyone.

Soon afterwards the great ship came sailing in, and the godless woman appeared before her father with a troubled countenance. He said, "Why dost thou come back alone? Where is thy husband?"

"Ah, dear father," she replied, "I come home again in great grief. During the voyage, my husband became suddenly ill and died, and if the good skipper had not given me his help, it would have gone ill with me. He was present at his death and can tell you all."

The king said, "I will make the dead alive again," and opened the chamber and bade the two come out. When the woman saw her husband, she was thunderstruck, and fell on her knees and begged for mercy. The king said, "There is no mercy. He was ready to die with thee and restored thee to life again, but thou hast murdered him in his sleep and shalt receive the reward that thou deservest." Then she was placed with her accomplice in a ship, which had been pierced with holes, and sent out to sea, where they soon sank amid the waves.

# The White Snake

LONG TIME AGO THERE LIVED A KING WHO WAS famed for his wisdom through all the land. Nothing was hidden from him, and it seemed as if news of the most secret things was brought to him through the air. But he had a strange custom. Every day after dinner, when the table was cleared and no one else was present, a trusty servant had to bring him one more dish. It was covered, however, and even the servant did not know what was in it; neither did anyone know, for the king never took off the cover to eat of it until he was quite alone.

This had gone on for a long time, when one day the servant, who took away the dish, was overcome with such curiosity that he could not help carrying the dish into his room. When he had carefully locked the door, he lifted up the cover and saw a white snake lying on the dish. But when he saw it, he could not deny himself the pleasure of tasting it, so he cut off a little bit and put it into his mouth. No sooner had it touched his tongue than he heard a strange whispering of little voices outside his window. He went and listened, and then noticed that it was the sparrows who were chattering together and telling one another of all kinds of things which they had seen in the fields and woods. Eating the snake had given him power of understanding the language of animals.

Now it so happened that on this very day the queen lost her most beautiful ring, and suspicion of having stolen it fell upon this trusty servant, who was allowed to go everywhere. The king ordered the man to be brought before him, and threatened with angry words that unless he could before the morrow point out the thief, he himself should be looked upon as guilty and executed. In vain he declared his innocence; he was dismissed with no better answer.

In his trouble and fear he went down into the courtyard and took thought how to help himself out of his trouble. Now some ducks were sitting together quietly by a brook and taking their rest; and, whilst they were making their feathers smooth with their bills, they were having a confidential conversation together. The servant stood by and listened. They were telling one another of all the places where they had been waddling about all the morning and what good food they had found; and one said in a pitiful tone, "Something lies heavy on my stomach; as I was eating in haste I swallowed a ring which lay under the queen's window."

The servant at once seized her by the neck, carried her to the kitchen, and said to the cook, "Here is a fine duck; pray, kill her."

"Yes," said the cook, and weighed her in his hand, "she has spared no trouble to fatten herself and has been waiting to be roasted long enough." So he cut off her head, and as she was being dressed for the spit, the queen's ring was found inside her.

The servant could now easily prove his innocence; and the king, to make amends for the wrong, allowed him to ask a favor and promised him the best place in the court that he could wish for. The servant refused everything, and only asked for a horse and some money for traveling, as he had a mind to see the world and go about a little.

When his request was granted, he set out on his way, and one day came to a pond, where he saw three fishes caught in the reeds and gasping for water. Now, though it is said that fishes are dumb, he heard them lamenting that they must perish so miserably, and, as he had a kind heart, he got off his horse and put the three prisoners back into the water. They quivered with delight, put out their heads, and cried to him, "We will remember you and repay you for saving us!"

He rode on, and after a while it seemed to him that he heard a voice in the sand at his feet. He listened, and heard an ant king complain, "Why cannot folks, with their clumsy beasts, keep off our bodies? That stupid horse, with his heavy hoofs, has been treading down my people without mercy!" So he turned on to a side path and the ant king cried out to him, "We will remember you—one good turn deserves another!"

The path led him into a wood, and here he saw two old ravens standing by their nest and throwing out their young ones. "Out with you, you idle, good-for-nothing creatures!" cried they. "We cannot find food for you any longer; you are big enough and can provide for yourselves."

But the poor young ravens lay upon the ground, flapping their wings and crying, "Oh, what helpless chicks we are! We must shift for ourselves, and yet we cannot fly! What can we do but lie here and starve?" So the good young fellow alighted and killed his horse with his sword, and gave it to them for food. Then they came hopping up to it, satisfied their hunger, and cried, "We will remember you—one good turn deserves another!"

And now he had to use his own legs, and when he had walked a long way, he came to a large city. There was a great noise and crowd in the streets, and a man rode up on horseback, crying aloud, "The king's daughter wants a husband; but whoever sues for her hand must perform a hard task, and if he does not succeed, he will forfeit his life." Many had already made the attempt but in vain; nevertheless when the youth saw the king's daughter he was so overcome by her great beauty that he forgot all danger, went before the king, and declared himself a suitor.

So he was led out to the sea, and a gold ring was thrown into it in his sight; then the king ordered him to fetch this ring up from the bottom of the sea, and added, "If you come up again without it, you will be thrown in again and again until you perish amid the waves." All the people grieved for the handsome youth; then they went away, leaving him alone by the sea.

He stood on the shore and considered what he should do, when suddenly he saw three fishes come swimming towards him, and they were the very fishes whose lives he had saved. The one in the middle held a mussel in its mouth, which it laid on the shore at the youth's feet; and when he had taken it up and opened it, there lay the gold ring in the shell. Full of joy he took it to the king, and expected that he would grant him the promised reward.

But when the proud princess perceived that he was not her equal in birth, she scorned him and required him first to perform another task. She went down into the garden and strewed with her own hands ten sacks full of millet seeds on the grass; then she said, "Tomorrow morning before sunrise these must be picked up and not a single grain be wanting."

The youth sat down in the garden and considered how it might be possible to perform this task, but he could think of nothing; and there he sat sorrowfully awaiting the break of day, when he should be led to death. But as soon as the first rays of the sun shone into the garden, he saw all the ten sacks standing side by side, quite full, and not a single grain was missing. The ant king had come in the night with thousands and thousands of ants, and the grateful creatures had by great industry picked up all the millet seeds and gathered them into the sacks.

Presently the king's daughter herself came down into the garden, and was amazed to see that the young man had done the task she had given him. But she could not yet conquer her proud heart, and said, "Although he has performed both the tasks, he shall not be my husband until he has brought me an apple from the Tree of Life."

The youth did not know where the Tree of Life stood, but he set out, and would have gone on forever, as long as his legs would carry him, though he had no hope of finding it. After he had wandered through three kingdoms, he came one evening to a wood, and lay down under a tree to sleep. But he heard a rustling in the branches, and a golden apple fell into his hand. At the same time three ravens flew down to him, perched themselves upon his knees, and said, "We are the three young ravens whom you saved from starving; when we had grown big, and heard that you were seeking the Golden Apple, we flew over the sea to the end of the world, where the Tree of Life stands, and have brought you the apple." The youth, full of joy, set out homewards, and took the Golden Apple to the king's beautiful daughter, who had no more excuses left to make. They cut the Apple of Life in two and ate it together; and then her heart became full of love for him, and they lived in undisturbed happiness to a great age.

TREE of LIFE

# The Straw, the Coal, and the Bean

N A VILLAGE DWELT A POOR OLD WOMAN, WHO had gathered together a dish of beans and wanted to cook them. So she made a fire on her hearth, and that it might burn the quicker, she lighted it with a handful of straw. When she was emptying the beans into the pan, one dropped without her observing it, and lay on the ground beside a straw; and soon afterwards a burning coal from the fire leapt down to the two. Then the straw began and said, "Dear friends, from whence do you come here?"

The coal replied, "I fortunately sprang out of the fire; and if I had not escaped by main force, my death would have been certain—I should have been burnt to ashes."

The bean said, "I, too, have escaped with a whole skin; but if the old woman had got me into the pan, I should have been made into broth without

any mercy, like my comrades."

"And would a better fate have fallen to my lot?" said the straw. "The old woman has destroyed all my brethren in fire and smoke; she seized sixty of them at once and took their lives. I luckily slipped through her fingers."

"But what are we to do now?" said the coal.

"I think," answered the bean, "that as we have so fortunately escaped death, we should keep together like good companions, and lest a new mischance should overtake us here, we should go away together and repair to a foreign country."

The proposition pleased the two others, and they set out on their way in company. Soon, however, they came to a little brook; and as there was no bridge or foot-plank, they did not know how they were to get over it. The straw hit on a good idea, and said, "I will lay myself straight across, and then you can walk over on me as on a bridge." The straw therefore stretched itself from one bank to the other, and the coal, who was of an impetuous disposition, tripped quite boldly on to the newly built bridge. But when she had reached the middle, and heard the water rushing beneath her, she was, after all, afraid, and stood still, and ventured no farther. The straw, however, began to burn, broke in two pieces, and fell into the stream. The coal slipped after her, hissed when she got into the water, and breathed her last. The bean, who had prudently stayed behind on the shore, could not but laugh at the event, was unable to stop, and laughed so heartily that she burst. It would have been all over with her, likewise, if, by good fortune, a tailor, who was traveling in search of work, had not sat down to rest by the brook. As he had a compassionate heart he pulled out his needle and thread, and sewed her together. The bean thanked him most prettily, but as the tailor used black thread, all beans since then have a black seam.

# The Fisherman and His Wife

HERE WAS ONCE ON A TIME A FISHERMAN WHO LIVED with his wife in a miserable hovel close by the sea, and every day he went out fishing. And once as he was sitting with his rod, looking at the clear water, his line suddenly went down, far down below, and when he drew it up again he brought out a large flounder. Then the flounder said to him, "Hark, you fisherman, I pray you, let me live. I am no flounder really but an enchanted prince. What good will it do you to kill me? I should not be good to eat. Put me in the water again, and let me go."

"Come," said the fisherman, "there is no need for so many words about it—a fish that can talk I should certainly let go, anyhow"; with that he put him back again into the clear water, and the flounder went to the bottom, leaving a long streak of blood behind him. Then the fisherman got up and went home to his wife in the hovel.

"Husband," said the woman, "have you caught nothing today?"

"No," said the man, "I did catch a flounder, who said he was an enchanted prince, so I let him go again."

"Did you not wish for anything first?" said the woman.

"No," said the man; "what should I wish for?"

"Ah," said the woman, "it is surely hard to have to live always in this dirty hovel; you might have wished for a small cottage for us. Go back and call him. Tell him we want to have a small cottage; he will certainly give us that."

"Ah," said the man, "why should I go there again?"

"Why," said the woman, "you did catch him, and you let him go again; he is sure to do it. Go at once." The man still did not quite like to go, but did not like to oppose his wife, and went to the sea.

When he got there, the sea was all green and yellow, and no longer so smooth; so he stood still and said,

*"Flounder, flounder in the sea,*
*Come, I pray thee, here to me;*
*For my wife, good Ilsabil,*
*Wills not as I'd have her will."*

Then the flounder came swimming to him and said, "Well, what does she want, then?"

"Ah," said the man, "I did catch you, and my wife says I really ought to have wished for something. She does not like to live in a wretched hovel any longer. She would like to have a cottage."

"Go, then," said the flounder, "she has it already."

When the man went home, his wife was no longer in the hovel, but instead of it there stood a small cottage, and she was sitting on a bench before the door. Then she took him by the hand and said to him, "Just come inside, look; now isn't this a great deal better?" So they went in, and there was a small porch and a pretty little parlor and bedroom, and a kitchen and pantry, with the best of furniture, and fitted up with the most beautiful things made of tin and brass, whatsoever was wanted. And behind the cottage there was a small yard, with hens and ducks, and a little garden with flowers and fruit. "Look," said the wife, "is not that nice!"

"Yes," said the husband, "and so we must always think it—now we will live quite contented."

"We will think about that," said the wife. With that they ate something and went to bed.

Everything went well for a week or a fortnight, and then the woman said, "Hark you, Husband, this cottage is far too small for us, and the garden and yard are little; the flounder might just as well have given us a larger house. I should like to live in a great stone castle; go to the flounder and tell him to give us a castle."

"Ah, Wife," said the man, "the cottage is quite good enough. Why should we live in a castle?"

"What!" said the woman. "Just go there; the flounder can always do that."

"No, Wife," said the man. "The flounder has just given us the cottage. I do not like to go back so soon; it might make him angry."

"Go," said the woman. "He can do it quite easily, and will be glad to do it; just you go to him."

The man's heart grew heavy, and he would not go. He said to himself, "It is not right," and yet he went. And when he came to the sea, the water was quite purple and dark blue, and grey and thick, and no longer so green and yellow, but it was still quiet. And he stood there and said—

*"Flounder, flounder in the sea,*
*Come, I pray thee, here to me;*
*For my wife, good Ilsabil,*
*Wills not as I'd have her will."*

"Well, what does she want, then?" said the flounder.

"Alas," said the man, half scared, "she wants to live in a great stone castle."

"Go to it, then; she is standing before the door," said the flounder.

Then the man went away, intending to go home; but when he got there, he found a great stone palace, and his wife was just standing on the steps going in; and she took him by the hand and said, "Come in." So he went in with her, and in the castle was a great hall paved with marble, and many servants, who flung wide the doors. And the walls were all bright with beautiful hangings; and in the rooms were chairs and tables of pure gold; and crystal chandeliers hung from the ceiling; and all the rooms and bedrooms had carpets; and food and wine of the very best were standing on all the tables, so that they nearly broke down beneath it. Behind the house, too, there was a great courtyard, with stables for horses and cows and the very best of carriages; there was a magnificent large garden, too, with the most beautiful flowers and fruit trees, and a park quite half a mile long, in which were stags, deer, and hares, and everything that could be desired. "Come," said the woman, "isn't that beautiful?"

"Yes, indeed," said the man, "now let it be; and we will live in this beautiful castle and be content."

"We will consider about that," said the woman, "and sleep upon it."

Thereupon they went to bed.

Next morning the wife awoke first, and it was just daybreak, and from her bed she saw the beautiful country lying before her. Her husband was still stretching himself, so she poked him in the side with her elbow, and said, "Get up, Husband, and just peep out of the window. Look you, couldn't we be the king over all that land? Go to the flounder; we will be the king."

"Ah, Wife," said the man, "why should we be king? I do not want to be king."

"Well," said the wife, "if you won't be king, I will; go to the flounder, for I will be king."

"Ah, Wife," said the man, "why do you want to be king? I do not like to say that to him."

"Why not?" said the woman. "Go to him this instant; I must be king!"

So the man went, and was quite unhappy because his wife wished to be king. "It is not right; it is not right," thought he. He did not wish to go, but yet he went.

And when he came to the sea, it was quite dark grey, and the water heaved up from below and smelt putrid. Then he went and stood by it, and said,

*"Flounder, flounder in the sea,*
*Come, I pray thee, here to me;*
*For my wife, good Ilsabil,*
*Wills not as I'd have her will."*

"Well, what does she want, then?" said the flounder.

"Alas," said the man, "she wants to be king."

"Go to her; she is king already."

So the man went, and when he came to the palace, the castle had become much larger and had a great tower and magnificent ornaments; and the sentinel was standing before the door; and there were numbers of soldiers with kettledrums and trumpets. And when he went inside the house, everything was of real marble and gold, with velvet covers and great golden tassels. Then the doors of the hall were opened; and there was the court in all its splendor, and his wife was sitting on a high throne of gold and diamonds, with a great crown of gold on her head and a sceptre of pure gold and jewels in her hand; and on both sides of her stood her maids-in-waiting in a row, each of them always one head shorter than the last.

Then he went and stood before her, and said, "Ah, Wife, and now you are king."

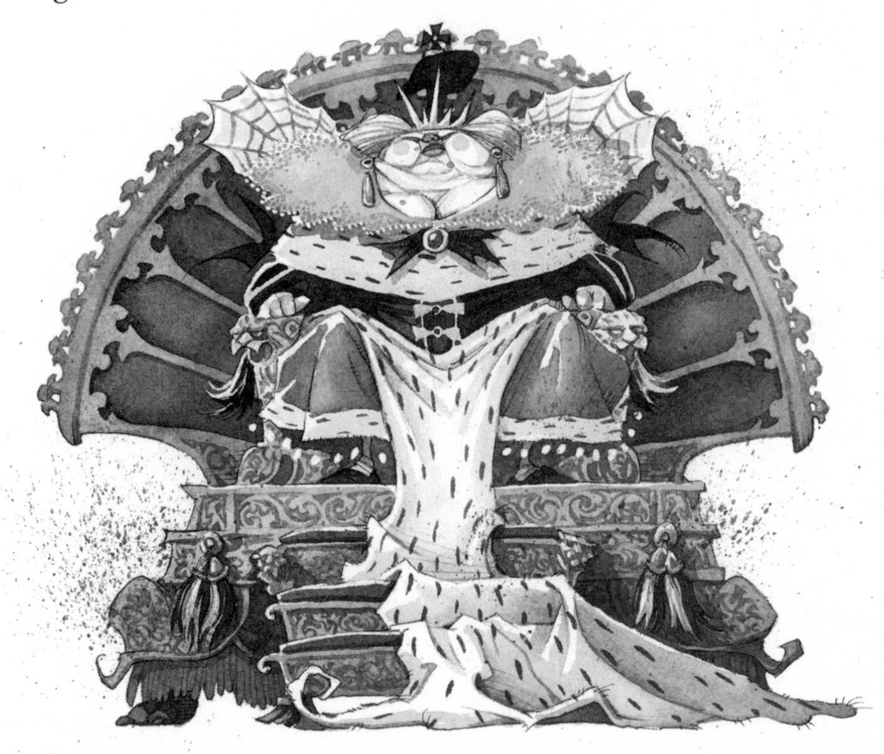

"Yes," said the woman, "now I am king."

So he stood and looked at her, and when he had looked at her thus for some time, he said, "And now that you are king, let all else be; now we will wish for nothing more."

"Nay, Husband," said the woman quite anxiously, "I find time passes very heavily; I can bear it no longer. Go to the flounder—I am king, but I must be emperor, too."

"Alas, Wife, why do you wish to be emperor?"

"Husband," said she, "go to the flounder. I will be emperor."

"Alas, Wife," said the man, "he cannot make you emperor; I may not say that to the fish. There is only one emperor in the land. An emperor the flounder cannot make you! I assure you he cannot."

"What!" said the woman. "I am the king, and you are nothing but my husband. Will you go this moment? Go at once! If he can make a king, he can make an emperor. I will be emperor; go instantly."

So he was forced to go. As the man went, however, he was troubled in mind and thought to himself, "It will not end well; it will not end well! Emperor is too shameless! The flounder will at last be tired out."

With that he reached the sea, and the sea was quite black and thick, and began to boil up from below so that it threw up bubbles; and such a sharp wind blew over it that it curdled, and the man was afraid. Then he went and stood by it, and said,

*"Flounder, flounder in the sea,*
*Come, I pray thee, here to me;*
*For my wife, good Ilsabil,*
*Wills not as I'd have her will."*

"Well, what does she want, then?" said the flounder.

"Alas, Flounder," said he, "my wife wants to be emperor."

"Go to her," said the flounder; "she is emperor already."

So the man went; and when he got there the whole palace was made of polished marble with alabaster figures and golden ornaments; and soldiers were marching before the door, blowing trumpets and beating cymbals and drums; and in the house, barons and counts and dukes were going about as servants. Then they opened the doors to him, which were of pure gold. And when he entered, there sat his wife on a throne, which was made of one piece of gold and was quite two miles high; and she wore a great golden crown that was three yards high and set with diamonds and carbuncles; and in one hand she had the sceptre and in the other the imperial orb; and on both sides of her stood the yeomen of the guard in two rows, each being smaller than the one before him, from the biggest giant, who was two miles high, to the very smallest dwarf, just as big as my little finger. And before it stood a number of princes and dukes.

Then the man went and stood among them, and said, "Wife, are you emperor now?"

"Yes," said she, "now I am emperor."

Then he stood and looked at her well, and when he had looked at her thus for some time, he said, "Ah, Wife, be content now that you are emperor."

"Husband," said she, "why are you standing there? Now I am emperor, but I will be pope too; go to the flounder."

"Alas, Wife," said the man, "what will you not wish for? You cannot be pope. There is but one in Christendom. He cannot make you pope."

"Husband," said she, "I will be pope; go immediately. I must be pope this very day."

"No, Wife," said the man. "I do not like to say that to him. That would not do, it is too much; the flounder can't make you pope."

"Husband," said she, "what nonsense! If he can make an emperor, he can make a pope. Go to him directly. I am emperor, and you are nothing but my husband; will you go at once?"

Then he was afraid and went; but he was quite faint, and shivered and shook, and his knees and legs trembled. And a high wind blew over the land, and the clouds flew, and towards evening all grew dark, and the leaves fell from the trees, and the water rose and roared as if it were boiling and splashed upon the shore. And in the distance he saw ships which were firing guns in their sore need, pitching and tossing on the waves. And yet in the midst of the sky there was still a small bit of blue, though on every side it was as red as in a heavy storm. So, full of despair, he went and stood in much fear and said,

*"Flounder, flounder in the sea,*
*Come, I pray thee, here to me;*
*For my wife, good Ilsabil,*
*Wills not as I'd have her will."*

"Well, what does she want, then?" said the flounder.

"Alas," said the man, "she wants to be pope."

"Go to her, then," said the flounder; "she is pope already."

So he went, and when he got there, he saw what seemed to be a large church surrounded by palaces. He pushed his way through the crowd. Inside, however, everything was lighted up with thousands and thousands of candles, and his wife was clad in gold, and she was sitting on a much higher throne and had three great golden crowns on, and round about her there was much ecclesiastical splendor; and on both sides of her was a row of candles the

largest of which was as tall as the very tallest tower, down to the very smallest kitchen candle; and all the emperors and kings were on their knees before her, kissing her shoe. "Wife," said the man, and looked attentively at her, "are you now pope?"

"Yes," said she, "I am pope." So he stood and looked at her, and it was just as if he were looking at the bright sun. When he had stood looking at her thus for a short time, he said, "Ah, Wife, if you are pope, do let well alone!" But she looked as stiff as a post and did not move or show any signs of life. Then said he, "Wife, now that you are pope, be satisfied; you cannot become anything greater now."

"I will consider about that," said the woman. Thereupon they both went to bed, but she was not satisfied, and greediness let her have no sleep, for she was continually thinking what there was left for her to be.

The man slept well and soundly, for he had run about a great deal during the day; but the woman could not fall asleep at all, and flung herself from one side to the other the whole night through, thinking always what more was left for her to be, but unable to call to mind anything else. At length the sun began to rise, and when the woman saw the red of dawn, she sat up in bed and looked at it. And when, through the window, she saw the sun thus rising, she said, "Cannot I, too, order the sun and moon to rise? Husband," she said, poking him in the ribs with her elbows, "wake up! Go to the flounder, for I wish to be even as God is."

The man was still half asleep, but he was so horrified that he fell out of bed. He thought he must have heard amiss, and rubbed his eyes and said, "Alas, Wife, what are you saying?"

"Husband," said she, "if I can't order the sun and moon to rise, and have to look on and see the sun and moon rising, I can't bear it. I shall not know what it is to have another happy hour, unless I can make them rise myself." Then she looked at him so terribly that a shudder ran over him, and said, "Go at once; I wish to be like unto God."

"Alas, Wife," said the man, falling on his knees before her, "the flounder cannot do that; he can make an emperor and a pope. I beseech you, go on as you are, and be pope."

Then she fell into a rage, and her hair flew wildly about her head, and she cried, "I will not endure this, I'll not bear it any longer; wilt thou go?"

Then he put on his trousers and ran away like a madman. But outside a great storm was raging and blowing so hard that he could scarcely keep his feet. Houses and trees toppled over, the mountains trembled, rocks rolled into the sea, the sky was pitch-black; and it thundered and lightninged and the sea came in with black waves as high as church towers and mountains, and all with crests of white foam at the top. Then he cried, but could not hear his own words,

*"Flounder, flounder in the sea,*
*Come, I pray thee, here to me;*
*For my wife, good Ilsabil,*
*Wills not as I'd have her will."*

"Well, what does she want, then?" said the flounder.

"Alas," said he, "she wants to be like unto God."

"Go to her, and you will find her back again in the dirty hovel."

And there they are living still at this very time.

# Cinderella

HE WIFE OF A RICH MAN FELL SICK, AND AS SHE FELT that her end was drawing near, she called her only daughter to her bedside and said, "Dear child, be good and pious, and then the good God will always protect thee, and I will look down on thee from heaven and be near thee." Thereupon she closed her eyes and departed.

Every day the maiden went out to her mother's grave and wept, and she remained pious and good. When winter came the snow spread a white sheet over the grave, and when the spring sun had drawn it off again, the man had taken another wife.

The woman had brought two daughters into the house with her, who were beautiful and fair of face but vile and black of heart. Now began a bad time for the poor stepchild. "Is the stupid goose to sit in the parlor with us?" said they. "He who wants to eat bread must earn it; out with the kitchen wench." They took her pretty clothes away from her, put an old grey bedgown on her, and gave her wooden shoes. "Just look at the proud princess, how decked out she is!" they cried, and laughed, and led her into the kitchen. There she had to do hard work from morning till night, get up before daybreak, carry water, light fires, cook, and wash. Besides this, the sisters did her every imaginable injury—they mocked her and emptied her peas and lentils into the ashes, so that she was forced to sit and pick them out again. In the evening when she had worked till she was weary, she had no bed to go to but had to sleep by the fireside in the ashes. And as on that account she always looked dusty and dirty, they called her Cinderella. It happened that the father was once going to the fair, and he asked his two stepdaughters what he should bring back for them. "Beautiful dresses," said one.

"Pearls and jewels," said the second.

"And thou, Cinderella," said he, "what wilt thou have?"

"Father, break off for me the first branch which knocks against your hat on your way home." So he bought beautiful dresses, pearls, and jewels for his two stepdaughters, and on his way home, as he was riding through a green thicket, a hazel twig brushed against him and knocked off his hat. Then he broke off the branch and took it with him. When he reached home, he gave his stepdaughters the things which they had wished for, and to Cinderella he gave the branch from the hazel bush. Cinderella thanked him, went to her mother's grave, and planted the branch on it, and wept so much that the tears fell down on it and watered it. And it grew, however, and became a handsome tree. Thrice a day Cinderella went and sat beneath it, and wept and prayed, and a little white bird always came on the tree, and if Cinderella expressed a wish, the bird threw down to her what she had wished for.

It happened, however, that the king appointed a festival which was to last three days, and to which all the beautiful young girls in the country were invited, in order that his son might choose himself a bride. When the two stepsisters heard that they, too, were to appear among the number, they were delighted, called Cinderella, and said, "Comb our hair for us, brush our shoes, and fasten our buckles, for we are going to the festival at the king's palace." Cinderella obeyed, but wept, because she, too, would have liked to go with them to the dance, and begged her stepmother to allow her to do so.

"Thou go, Cinderella!" said she. "Thou art dusty and dirty and wouldst go to the festival? Thou hast no clothes and shoes, and yet wouldst dance!" As, however, Cinderella went on asking, the stepmother at last said, "I have emptied a dish of lentils into the ashes for thee; if thou hast picked them out again in two hours, thou shalt go with us."

The maiden went through the back door into the garden, and called, "You tame pigeons, you turtledoves, and all you birds beneath the sky, come and help me to pick

*The good into the pot,*
*The bad into the crop."*

Then two white pigeons came in by the kitchen window, and afterwards the turtledoves and at last all the birds beneath the sky came whirring and crowding in and alighted amongst the ashes. And the pigeons nodded with their heads and began *pick, pick, pick, pick*, and the rest began also *pick, pick, pick, pick*, and gathered all the good grains into the dish. Hardly had one hour passed before they had finished, and all flew out again. Then the girl took the dish to her stepmother, and was glad, and believed that now she would be allowed to go with them to the festival. But the stepmother said, "No, Cinderella, thou hast no clothes and thou canst not dance; thou wouldst only be laughed at." And as Cinderella wept at this, the stepmother said, "If thou canst pick two dishes of lentils out of the ashes for me in one hour, thou shalt go with us." And she thought to herself, "That she most certainly cannot do."

When the stepmother had emptied the two dishes of lentils amongst the ashes, the maiden went through the back door into the garden and cried, "You tame pigeons, you turtledoves, and all you birds under heaven come and help me to pick

*The good into the pot,*
*The bad into the crop."*

Then two white pigeons came in by the kitchen window, and afterwards the turtledoves, and at length all the birds beneath the sky came whirring and crowding in and alighted amongst the ashes. And the doves nodded with their heads and began *pick, pick, pick, pick,* and the others began also *pick, pick, pick, pick,* and gathered all the good seeds into the dishes, and before half an hour was over they had already finished, and all flew out again. Then the maiden carried the dishes to the stepmother and was delighted, and believed that she might now go with them to the festival. But the stepmother said, "All this will not help thee; thou goest not with us, for thou hast no clothes and canst not dance; we should be ashamed of thee!" On this she turned her back on Cinderella, and hurried away with her two proud daughters.

As no one was now at home, Cinderella went to her mother's grave beneath the hazel tree, and cried,

*"Shiver and quiver, little tree,*
*Silver and gold throw down over me."*

Then the bird threw a gold and silver dress down to her, and slippers embroidered with silk and silver. She put on the dress with all speed and went to the festival. Her stepsisters and the stepmother, however, did not know her and thought she must be a foreign princess, for she looked so beautiful in the golden dress. They never once thought of Cinderella, and believed that she was sitting at home in the dirt, picking lentils out of the ashes. The prince went to meet her, took her by the hand, and danced with her. He would dance with no other maiden, and never let loose of her hand; and if anyone else came to invite her, he said, "This is my partner."

She danced till it was evening, and then she wanted to go home. But the king's son said, "I will go with thee and bear thee company," for he wished to see to whom the beautiful maiden belonged. She escaped from him, however, and sprang into the pigeon house. The king's son waited until her father came, and then he told him that the stranger maiden had leapt into the pigeon house.

The old man thought, "Can it be Cinderella?" and they had to bring him an axe and a pickaxe that he might hew the pigeon house to pieces, but no one was inside it. And when they got home, Cinderella lay in her dirty clothes among the ashes, and a dim little oil lamp was burning on the mantelpiece, for Cinderella had jumped quickly down from the back of the pigeon house and had run to the little hazel tree, and there she had taken off her beautiful clothes and laid them on the grave, and the bird had taken them away again; and then she had placed herself in the kitchen amongst the ashes in her grey gown.

Next day when the festival began afresh, and her parents and the stepsisters had gone once more, Cinderella went to the hazel tree and said—

*"Shiver and quiver, my little tree,*
*Silver and gold throw down over me."*

Then the bird threw down a much more beautiful dress than on the preceding day. And when Cinderella appeared at the festival in this dress, everyone was astonished at her beauty. The king's son had waited until she came, and instantly took her by the hand and danced with no one but her. When others came and invited her, he said, "She is my partner." When evening came she wished to leave, and the king's son followed her and wanted to see into which house she went. But she sprang away from him and into the garden behind the house. Therein stood a beautiful tall tree on which hung the most magnificent pears. She clambered so nimbly between the branches like a squirrel that the king's son did not know where she was gone. He waited until her father came, and said to him, "The stranger maiden has escaped from me, and I believe she has climbed up the pear tree."

The father thought, "Can it be Cinderella?" and had an axe brought and cut the tree down, but no one was on it. And when they got into the kitchen, Cinderella lay there amongst the ashes, as usual, for she had jumped down on the other side of the tree, had taken the beautiful dress to the bird on the little hazel tree, and put on her grey gown.

On the third day, when the parents and sisters had gone away, Cinderella went once more to her mother's grave and said to the little tree—

*"Shiver and quiver, my little tree,*
*Silver and gold throw down over me."*

And now the bird threw down to her a dress which was more splendid and magnificent than any she had yet had, and the slippers were golden. And when she went to the festival in the dress, no one knew how to speak for astonishment. The king's son danced with her only, and if anyone invited her to dance, he said, "She is my partner."

When evening came, Cinderella wished to leave, and the king's son was anxious to go with her, but she escaped from him so quickly that he could not follow her. The king's son had, however, used a stratagem, and had caused the whole staircase to be smeared with pitch, and there, when she ran down, had the maiden's left slipper remained sticking. The king's son picked it up, and it was small and dainty, and all golden.

Next morning, he went with it to the father, and said to him, "No one shall be my wife but she whose foot this golden slipper fits." Then were the two sisters glad, for they had pretty feet. The eldest went with the shoe into her room and wanted to try it on, and her mother stood by. But she could not get her big toe into it, and the shoe was too small for her. Then her mother gave

her a knife and said, "Cut the toe off; when thou art queen thou wilt have no more need to go on foot." The maiden cut the toe off, forced the foot into the shoe, swallowed the pain, and went out to the king's son. Then he took her on his horse as his bride and rode away with her. They were, however, obliged to pass the grave, and there, on the hazel tree, sat the two pigeons and cried,

*"Turn and peep, turn and peep,*
*There's blood within the shoe,*
*The shoe it is too small for her,*
*The true bride waits for you."*

Then he looked at her foot and saw how the blood was streaming from it. He turned his horse round and took the false bride home again, and said she was not the true one, and that the other sister was to put the shoe on. Then this one went into her chamber and got her toes safely into the shoe, but her heel was too large. So her mother gave her a knife and said, "Cut a bit off thy heel; when thou art queen thou wilt have no more need to go on foot." The maiden cut a bit off her heel, forced her foot into the shoe, swallowed the pain, and went out to the king's son. He took her on his horse as his bride and rode away with her, but when they passed by the hazel tree, two little pigeons sat on it and cried,

*"Turn and peep, turn and peep,*
*There's blood within the shoe*
*The shoe it is too small for her,*
*The true bride waits for you."*

He looked down at her foot and saw how the blood was running out of her shoe, and how it had stained her white stocking. Then he turned his horse and took the false bride home again. "This also is not the right one," said he.

"Have you no other daughter?"

"No," said the man. "There is still a little stunted kitchen wench which my late wife left behind her, but she cannot possibly be the bride."

The king's son said he was to send her up to him; but the mother answered, "Oh, no, she is much too dirty; she cannot show herself!" He absolutely insisted on it, and Cinderella had to be called. She first washed her hands and face clean, and then went and bowed down before the king's son, who gave her the golden shoe. Then she seated herself on a stool, drew her foot out of the heavy wooden shoe, and put it into the slipper, which fitted like a glove.

And when she rose up and the king's son looked at her face, he recognized the beautiful maiden who had danced with him and cried, "That is the true bride!" The stepmother and the two sisters were terrified and became pale with rage; he, however, took Cinderella on his horse and rode away with her. As they passed by the hazel tree, the two white doves cried—

*"Turn and peep, turn and peep,*
*No blood is in the shoe,*
*The shoe is not too small for her,*
*The true bride rides with you,"*

and when they had cried that, the two came flying down and placed themselves on Cinderella's shoulders, one on the right, the other on the left, and remained sitting there.

When the wedding with the king's son had to be celebrated, the two false sisters came and wanted to get into favor with Cinderella and share her good fortune. When the betrothed couple went to church, the elder was at the right side and the younger at the left, and the pigeons pecked out one eye of each of them. Afterwards as they came back, the elder was at the left and the younger at the right, and then the pigeons pecked out the other eye of each. And thus, for their wickedness and falsehood, they were punished with blindness as long as they lived.

# The Three Little Men in the Forest

HERE WAS ONCE A MAN WHOSE WIFE DIED AND A woman whose husband died; and the man had a daughter, and the woman also had a daughter. The girls were acquainted with each other and went out walking together, and afterwards came to the woman in her house. Then said she to the man's daughter, "Listen, tell thy father that I would like to marry him, and then thou shalt wash thyself in milk every morning and drink wine, but my own daughter shall wash herself in water and drink water."

The girl went home and told her father what the woman had said. The man said, "What shall I do? Marriage is a joy and also a torment." At length as he could come to no decision, he pulled off his boot, and said, "Take this boot; it has a hole in the sole of it. Go with it up to the loft, hang it on the big nail, and then pour water into it. If it hold the water, then I will again take a wife; but

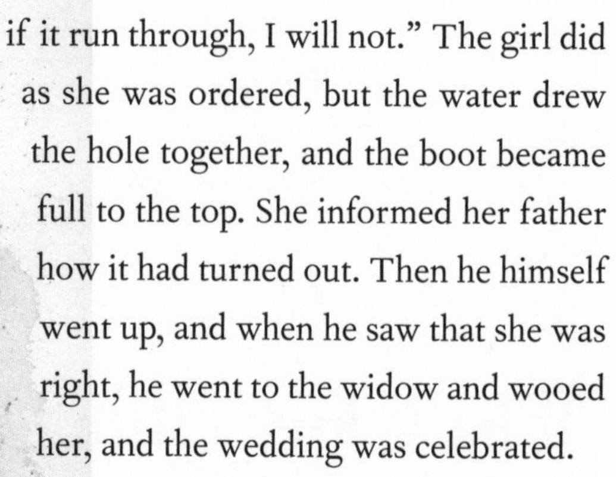

if it run through, I will not." The girl did as she was ordered, but the water drew the hole together, and the boot became full to the top. She informed her father how it had turned out. Then he himself went up, and when he saw that she was right, he went to the widow and wooed her, and the wedding was celebrated.

The next morning, when the two girls got up, there stood before the man's daughter milk for her to wash in and wine for her to drink, but before the woman's daughter stood water to wash herself with and water for drinking. On the second morning stood water for washing and water for drinking before the man's daughter as well as before the woman's daughter. And on the third morning stood water for washing and water for drinking before the man's daughter, and milk for washing and wine for drinking before the woman's daughter, and so it continued. The woman became bitterly unkind to her stepdaughter, and day by day did her best to treat her still worse. She was also envious because her stepdaughter was beautiful and lovable, and her own daughter ugly and repulsive.

Once, in winter, when everything was frozen as hard as a stone, and hill and vale lay covered with snow, the woman made a frock of paper, called her stepdaughter, and said, "Here, put on this dress and go out into the wood and fetch me a little basketful of strawberries—I have a fancy for some."

"Good heavens!" said the girl. "No strawberries grow in winter! The ground is frozen, and besides the snow has covered everything. And why am I to go in this paper frock? It is so cold outside that one's very breath freezes! The wind will blow through the frock, and the thorns will tear it off my body."

"Wilt thou contradict me again?" said the stepmother. "See that thou goest, and do not show thy face again until thou hast the basketful of strawberries!" Then she gave her a little piece of hard bread, and said, "This will last thee the day," and thought, "Thou wilt die of cold and hunger outside and wilt never be seen again by me."

Then the maiden was obedient and put on the paper frock and went out with the basket. Far and wide there was nothing but snow, and not a green blade to be seen. When she got into the wood she saw a small house out of which peeped three little men. She wished them good day, and knocked modestly at the door. They cried, "Come in," and she entered the room and seated herself on the bench by the stove, where she began to warm herself and eat her breakfast. The little men said, "Give us, too, some of it."

"Willingly," she said, and divided her bit of bread in two and gave them the half.

They asked, "What dost thou here in the forest in the wintertime in thy thin dress?"

"Ah," she answered, "I am to look for a basketful of strawberries, and am not to go home until I can take them with me."

When she had eaten her bread, they gave her a broom and said, "Sweep away the snow at the back door with it." But when she was outside, the three little men said to one another, "What shall we give her as she is so good and has shared her bread with us?"

Then said the first, "My gift is that she shall every day grow more beautiful."

The second said, "My gift is that gold pieces shall fall out of her mouth every time she speaks."

The third said, "My gift is that a king shall come and take her to wife."

The girl, however, did as the little men had bidden her, swept away the snow behind the little house with the broom, and what did she find but real ripe strawberries, which came up quite dark red out of the snow! In her joy she hastily gathered her basket full, thanked the little men, shook hands with each of them, and ran home to take her stepmother what she had longed for so much.

When she went in and said good evening, a piece of gold at once fell from her mouth. Thereupon she related what had happened to her in the wood, but with every word she spoke, gold pieces fell from her mouth until very soon the whole room was covered with them.

"Now look at her arrogance," cried the stepsister, "to throw about gold in that way!" But she was secretly envious of it and wanted to go into the forest also to seek strawberries.

The mother said, "No, my dear little daughter, it is too cold; thou mightest die of cold." However, as her daughter let her have no peace, the mother at last yielded, made her a magnificent dress of fur, which she was obliged to put on, and gave her bread and butter and cake to take with her.

The girl went into the forest and straight up to the little house. The three little men peeped out again, but she did not greet them; and without looking round at them and without speaking to them, she went awkwardly into the room, seated herself by the stove, and began to eat her bread and butter and cake.

"Give us some of it," cried the little men.

But she replied, "There is not enough for myself, so how can I give it away to other people?"

When she had done eating, they said, "There is a broom for thee; sweep all clean for us outside by the back door."

"Humph! Sweep for yourselves," she answered. "I am not your servant." When she saw that they were not going to give her anything, she went out by the door.

Then the little men said to one another, "What shall we give her as she is so naughty and has a wicked envious heart that will never let her do a good turn to anyone?"

The first said, "I grant that she may grow uglier every day."

The second said, "I grant that at every word she says, a toad shall spring out of her mouth."

The third said, "I grant that she may die a miserable death."

The maiden looked for strawberries outside, but as she found none, she went angrily home. And when she opened her mouth and was about to tell her mother what had happened to her in the wood, with every word she said, a toad sprang out of her mouth, so that everyone was seized with horror of her.

Then the stepmother was still more enraged and thought of nothing but how to do every possible injury to the man's daughter, whose beauty, however, grew daily greater. At length she took a cauldron, set it on the fire, and boiled yarn in it. When it was boiled, she flung it on the poor girl's shoulder and gave her an axe in order that she might go on the frozen river, cut a hole in the ice, and rinse the yarn.

She was obedient, went thither, and cut a hole in the ice; and while she was in the midst of her cutting, a splendid carriage came driving up, in which sat the king. The carriage stopped, and the king asked, "My child, who are thou, and what art thou doing here?"

"I am a poor girl, and I am rinsing yarn."

Then the king felt compassion, and when he saw that she was so very beautiful, he said to her, "Wilt thou go away with me?"

"Ah, yes, with all my heart," she answered, for she was glad to get away from the mother and sister.

So she got into the carriage and drove away with the king, and when they arrived at his palace, the wedding was celebrated with great pomp, as the little men had granted to the maiden. When a year was over, the young queen bore a son, and as the stepmother had heard of her great good fortune, she came with her daughter to the palace and pretended that she wanted to pay her a visit. Once, however, when the king had gone out, and no one else was

present, the wicked woman seized the queen by the head, and her daughter seized her by the feet, and they lifted her out of the bed and threw her out of the window into the stream which flowed by. Then the ugly daughter laid herself in the bed, and the old woman covered her up over her head.

When the king came home again and wanted to speak to his wife, the old woman cried, "Hush, hush, that can't be now; she is lying in a violent perspiration. You must let her rest today."

The king suspected no evil, and did not come back again till next morning; and as he talked with his wife and she answered him, with every word a toad leapt out, whereas formerly a piece of gold had fallen out. Then he asked what that could be, but the old woman said that she had got that from the violent perspiration and would soon lose it again. During the night, however, the scullion saw a duck come swimming up the gutter, and it said,

*"King, what art thou doing now?*
*Sleepest thou, or wakest thou?"*

And as he returned no answer, it said,

*"And my guests, what may they do?"*

The scullion said,

*"They are sleeping soundly, too."*

Then it asked again,

*"What does little baby mine?"*

He answered,

*"Sleepeth in his cradle fine."*

Then she went upstairs in the form of the queen, nursed the baby, shook up its little bed, covered it over, and then swam away again down the gutter in the shape of a duck. She came thus for two nights. On the third, she said to the scullion, "Go and tell the king to take his sword and swing it three times over me on the threshold."

Then the scullion ran and told this to the king, who came with his sword and swung it thrice over the spirit; and at the third time, his wife stood before him strong, living, and healthy as she had been before. Thereupon the king was full of great joy, but he kept the queen hidden in a chamber until the Sunday, when the baby was to be christened. And when it was christened, he said, "What does a person deserve who drags another out of bed and throws him in the water?"

"The wretch deserves nothing better," answered the old woman, "than to be taken and put in a barrel stuck full of nails and rolled downhill into the water."

"Then," said the king, "thou hast pronounced thine own sentence"; and he ordered such a barrel to be brought and the old woman to be put into it with her daughter, and then the top was hammered on and the barrel rolled downhill until it went into the river.

# The Mouse, the Bird, and the Sausage

NCE ON A TIME A MOUSE, A BIRD, AND A SAUSAGE became companions, kept house together, lived well and happily with one another, and wonderfully increased their possessions. The bird's work was to fly every day into the forest and bring back wood. The mouse had to carry water, light the fire, and lay the table; but the sausage had to cook.

He who is too well off is always longing for something new. One day, therefore, the bird met with another bird on the way to whom it related its excellent circumstances and boasted of them. The other bird, however, called it a poor simpleton for his hard work, but said that the two at home had good times. For when the mouse had made her fire and carried her water, she went into her little room to rest until they called her to lay the table. The sausage

stayed by the pot, saw that the food was cooking well; and, when it was nearly time for dinner, it rolled itself once or twice through the broth or vegetables and then they were buttered, salted, and ready. When the bird came home and laid his burden down, they sat down to dinner; and after they had had their meal, they slept their fill till next morning, and that was a splendid life.

Next day the bird, prompted by the other bird, would go no more into the wood, saying that he had been servant long enough, and had been made a fool of by them, and that they must change about for once and try to arrange it in another way. And though the mouse and the sausage also begged most earnestly, the bird would have his way and said it must be tried. They cast lots about it, and the lot fell on the sausage who was to carry wood, the mouse became cook, and the bird was to fetch water.

What happened? The little sausage went out towards the wood, the little bird lighted the fire, the mouse stayed by the pot and waited alone until little sausage came home and brought wood for next day. But the little sausage stayed so long on the road that they both feared something was amiss, and the bird flew out a little way in the air to meet it. Not far off, however, it met a dog on the road who had fallen on the poor sausage as lawful booty, and had seized and swallowed it. The bird charged the dog with an act of barefaced robbery, but it was in vain to speak, for the dog said he had found forged letters on the sausage, on which account its life was forfeited to him.

The bird sadly took up the wood, flew home, and related what he had seen and heard. They were much troubled, but agreed to do their best and remain together. The bird therefore laid the cloth, and the mouse made ready the food, and wanted to dress it, and to get into the pot as the sausage used to do, and roll and creep amongst the vegetables to mix them; but before she got into the midst of them, she was stopped, and lost her skin and hair and life in the attempt.

When the bird came to carry up the dinner, no cook was there. In its distress the bird threw the wood here and there, called and searched, but no cook was to be found! Owing to his carelessness the wood caught fire, so that a conflagration ensued, the bird hastened to fetch water, and then the bucket dropped from his claws into the well, and he fell down with it, and could not recover himself, but had to drown there.

# Clever Hans

HE MOTHER OF HANS SAID, "WHITHER AWAY, HANS?"

Hans answered, "To Gretel."

"Behave well, Hans."

"Oh, I'll behave well. Good-bye, Mother."

"Good-bye, Hans."

Hans comes to Gretel, "Good day, Gretel."

"Good day, Hans. What dost thou bring that is good?"

"I bring nothing. I want to have something given me." Gretel presents Hans with a needle. Hans says, "Good-bye, Gretel."

"Good-bye, Hans."

Hans takes the needle, sticks it into a hay-cart, and follows the cart home.

"Good evening, Mother."

"Good evening, Hans. Where hast thou been?"

"With Gretel."

"What didst thou take her?"

"Took nothing; had something given me."

"What did Gretel give thee?"

"Gave me a needle."

"Where is the needle, Hans?"

"Stuck it in the hay-cart."

"That was ill done, Hans. Thou shouldst have stuck the needle in thy sleeve."

"Never mind, I'll do better next time."

"Whither away, Hans?"

"To Gretel, Mother."

"Behave well, Hans."

"Oh, I'll behave well. Good-bye, Mother."

"Good-bye, Hans."

Hans comes to Gretel. "Good day, Gretel."

"Good day, Hans. What dost thou bring that is good?"

"I bring nothing; I want to have something given to me." Gretel presents Hans with a knife. "Good-bye, Gretel."

"Good-bye Hans." Hans takes the knife, sticks it in his sleeve, and goes home.

"Good evening, Mother."

"Good evening, Hans. Where hast thou been?"

"With Gretel."

"What didst thou take her?"

"Took her nothing; she gave me something."

"What did Gretel give thee?"

"Gave me a knife."

"Where is the knife, Hans?"

"Stuck in my sleeve."

"That's ill done, Hans. Thou shouldst have put the knife in thy pocket."

"Never mind, will do better next time."

"Whither away, Hans?"

"To Gretel, Mother."

"Behave well, Hans."

"Oh, I'll behave well. Good-bye, Mother."

"Good-bye, Hans."

Hans comes to Gretel. "Good day, Gretel."

"Good day, Hans. What good thing dost thou bring?"

"I bring nothing; I want something given me." Gretel presents Hans with a young goat. "Good-bye, Gretel."

"Good-bye, Hans." Hans takes the goat, ties its legs, and puts it in his pocket. When he gets home, it is suffocated.

"Good evening, Mother."

"Good evening, Hans. Where hast thou been?"

"With Gretel."

"What didst thou take her?"

"Took nothing; she gave me something."

"What did Gretel give thee?"

"She gave me a goat."

"Where is the goat, Hans?"

"Put it in my pocket."

"That was ill done, Hans. Thou shouldst have put a rope round the goat's neck."

"Never mind, will do better next time."

"Whither away, Hans?"

"To Gretel, Mother."

"Behave well, Hans."

"Oh, I'll behave well. Good-bye, Mother."

"Good-bye, Hans."

Hans comes to Gretel. "Good day, Gretel."

"Good day, Hans. What good thing dost thou bring?"

"I bring nothing; I want something given me." Gretel presents Hans with a piece of bacon. "Good-bye, Gretel."

"Good-bye, Hans."

Hans takes the bacon, ties it to a rope, and drags it away behind him. The dogs come and devour the bacon. When he gets home, he has the rope in his hand, and there is no longer anything hanging to it.

"Good evening, Mother."

"Good evening, Hans. Where hast thou been?"

"With Gretel."

"What didst thou take her?"

"I took her nothing; she gave me something."

"What did Gretel give thee?"

"Gave me a bit of bacon."

"Where is the bacon, Hans?"

"I tied it to a rope, brought it home; dogs took it."

"That was ill done, Hans. Thou shouldst have carried the bacon on thy head."

"Never mind, will do better next time."

"Whither away, Hans?"

"To Gretel, Mother."

"Behave well, Hans."

"I'll behave well. Good-bye, Mother."

"Good-bye, Hans."

Hans comes to Gretel. "Good day, Gretel."

"Good day, Hans. What good thing dost thou bring?"

"I bring nothing but would have something given."

Gretel presents Hans with a calf. "Good-bye, Gretel."

"Good-bye, Hans."

Hans takes the calf, puts it on his head, and the calf kicks his face.

"Good evening, Mother."

"Good evening, Hans. Where hast thou been?"

"With Gretel."

"What didst thou take her?"

"I took nothing but had something given me."

"What did Gretel give thee?"

"A calf."

"Where hast thou the calf, Hans?"

"I set it on my head and it kicked my face."

"That was ill done, Hans. Thou shouldst have led the calf and put it in the stall."

"Never mind, will do better next time."

"Whither away, Hans?"

"To Gretel, Mother."

"Behave well, Hans."

"I'll behave well. Good-bye, Mother."

"Good-bye, Hans."

Hans comes to Gretel. "Good day, Gretel."

"Good day, Hans. What good thing dost thou bring?"

"I bring nothing but would have something given."

Gretel says to Hans, "I will go with thee."

Hans takes Gretel, ties her to a rope, leads her to the rack, and binds her fast. Then Hans goes to his mother.

"Good evening, Mother."

"Good evening, Hans. Where hast thou been?"

"With Gretel."

"What didst thou take her?"

"I took her nothing."

"What did Gretel give thee?"

"She gave me nothing; she came with me."

"Where hast thou left Gretel?"

"I led her by the rope, tied her to the rack, and scattered some grass for her."

"That was ill done, Hans. Thou shouldst have cast friendly eyes on her."

"Never mind, will do better."

Hans went into the stable, cut out all the calves' and sheep's eyes, and threw them in Gretel's face. Then Gretel became angry, tore herself loose and ran away, and never became the bride of Hans.

# Little Red-Cap

NCE UPON A TIME THERE WAS A DEAR LITTLE GIRL who was loved by everyone who looked at her, but most of all by her grandmother, and there was nothing that she would not have given to the child. Once she gave her a little cap of red velvet, which suited her so well that she would never wear anything else; so she was always called "Little Red-Cap."

One day her mother said to her, "Come, Little Red-Cap, here is a piece of cake and a bottle of wine; take them to your grandmother. She is ill and weak, and they will do her good. Set out before it gets hot, and when you are going, walk nicely and quietly and do not run off the path, or you may fall and break the bottle, and then your grandmother will get nothing; and when you go into her room, don't forget to say 'Good morning,' and don't peep into every corner before you do it."

"I will take great care," said Little Red-Cap to her mother, and gave her hand on it.

The grandmother lived out in the wood, half a league from the village; and just as Little Red-Cap entered the wood, a wolf met her. Red-Cap did not know what a wicked creature he was and was not at all afraid of him.

"Good-day, Little Red-Cap," said he.

"Thank you kindly, wolf."

"Whither away so early, Little Red-Cap?"

"To my grandmother's."

"What have you got in your apron?"

"Cake and wine; yesterday was baking day, so poor sick grandmother is to have something good, to make her stronger."

"Where does your grandmother live, Little Red-Cap?"

"A good quarter of a league farther on in the wood; her house stands under the three large oak trees, the nut trees are just below; you surely must know it," replied Little Red-Cap.

The wolf thought to himself, "What a tender young creature! What a nice plump mouthful—she will be better to eat than the old woman. I must act

craftily, so as to catch both." So he walked for a short time by the side of Little Red-Cap, and then he said, "See, Little Red-Cap, how pretty the flowers are about here—why do you not look round? I believe, too, that you do not hear how sweetly the little birds are singing; you walk gravely along as if you were going to school, while everything else out here in the wood is merry."

Little Red-Cap raised her eyes, and when she saw the sunbeams dancing here and there through the trees, and pretty flowers growing everywhere, she thought, "Suppose I take grandmother a fresh nosegay; that would please her, too. It is so early in the day that I shall still get there in good time." And so she ran from the path into the wood to look for flowers. And whenever she had picked one, she fancied that she saw a still prettier one farther on, and ran after it, and so got deeper and deeper into the wood.

Meanwhile the wolf ran straight to the grandmother's house and knocked at the door.

"Who is there?"

"Little Red-Cap," replied the wolf. "She is bringing cake and wine; open the door."

"Lift the latch," called out the grandmother. "I am too weak and cannot get up."

The wolf lifted the latch, the door flew open, and without saying a word he went straight to the grandmother's bed and devoured her. Then he put on her clothes, dressed himself in her cap, laid himself in bed, and drew the curtains.

Little Red-Cap, however, had been running about picking flowers, and when she had gathered so many that she could carry no more, she remembered her grandmother, and set out on the way to her.

She was surprised to find the cottage door standing open, and when she went into the room, she had such a strange feeling that she said to herself, "Oh dear! How uneasy I feel today, and at other times I like being with grandmother so much." She called out, "Good morning," but received no answer; so she went to the bed and drew back the curtains. There lay her grandmother with her cap pulled far over her face, and looking very strange.

"Oh! Grandmother," she said, "what big ears you have!"

"The better to hear you with, my child" was the reply.

"But, Grandmother, what big eyes you have!" she said.

"The better to see you with, my dear."

"But, Grandmother, what large hands you have!"

"The better to hug you with."

"Oh! But, Grandmother, what a terrible big mouth you have!"

"The better to eat you with!"

And scarcely had the wolf said this, than with one bound he was out of bed and swallowed up Red-Cap.

When the wolf had appeased his appetite, he lay down again in the bed, fell asleep, and began to snore very loudly. The huntsman was just passing the house, and thought to himself, "How the old woman is snoring! I must just see if she wants anything." So he went into the room; and when he came to the bed, he saw that the wolf was lying in it. "Do I find thee here, thou old sinner!" said he. "I have long sought thee!" Then just as he was going to fire at him, it occurred to him that the wolf might have devoured the grandmother and that she might still be saved, so he did not fire but took a pair of scissors and began to cut open the stomach of the sleeping wolf.

When he had made two snips, he saw the little Red-Cap shining, and then he made two snips more, and the little girl sprang out, crying, "Ah, how

frightened I have been! How dark it was inside the wolf"; and after that the aged grandmother came out alive also but scarcely able to breathe. Red-Cap, however, quickly fetched great stones with which they filled the wolf's body, and when he awoke, he wanted to run away, but the stones were so heavy that he fell down at once, and fell dead.

Then all three were delighted. The huntsman drew off the wolf's skin and went home with it; the grandmother ate the cake and drank the wine which Red-Cap had brought, and revived; but Red-Cap thought to herself, "As long as I live, I will never by myself leave the path, to run into the wood, when my mother has forbidden me to do so."

It is also related that once when Red-Cap was again taking cakes to the old grandmother, another wolf spoke to her and tried to entice her from the path. Red-Cap, however, was on her guard and went straight forward on her way, and told her grandmother that she had met the wolf and that he had said good morning to her, but with such a wicked look in his eyes that if they had not been on the public road, she was certain he would have eaten her up.

"Well," said the grandmother, "we will shut the door that he may not come in."

Soon afterwards the wolf knocked, and cried, "Open the door, Grandmother. I am little Red-Cap and am fetching you some cakes."

But they did not speak or open the door, so the greybeard stole twice or thrice round the house, and at last jumped on the roof, intending to wait until Red-Cap went home in the evening and then to steal after her and devour her in the darkness.

But the grandmother saw what was in his thoughts. In front of the house was a great stone trough, so she said to the child, "Take the pail, Red-Cap; I made some sausages yesterday, so carry the water in which I boiled them to the trough." Red-Cap carried until the great trough was quite full. Then the smell of the sausages reached the wolf, and he sniffed and peeped down, and at last stretched out his neck so far that he could no longer keep his footing and began to slip, and slipped down from the roof straight into the great trough and was drowned. But Red-Cap went joyously home, and never did anything to harm anyone.

# The Seven Ravens

HERE WAS ONCE A MAN WHO HAD SEVEN SONS, AND still he had no daughter, however much he wished for one. At length his wife again gave him hope of a child, and when it came into the world it was a girl. The joy was great, but the child was sickly and small and had to be privately baptized on account of its weakness. The father sent one of the boys in haste to the spring to fetch water for the baptism. The other six went with him, and as each of them wanted to be first to fill it, the jug fell into the well. There they stood and did not know what to do, and none of them dared to go home. As they still did not return, the father grew impatient, and said, "They have certainly forgotten it for some game, the wicked boys!" He became afraid that the girl would have to die without being baptized, and in his anger cried, "I wish the boys were all turned into ravens." Hardly was the word spoken before he heard a whirring of wings over his head in the air, looked up, and saw seven coal-black ravens flying away. The parents could not recall the curse, and however sad they were at the loss of their seven sons, they still to some extent comforted themselves with their dear little daughter, who soon grew strong and every day became more beautiful.

For a long time she did not know that she had had brothers, for her parents were careful not to mention them before her; but one day she accidentally heard some people saying of herself, "That the girl was certainly beautiful, but that in reality she was to blame for the misfortune which had befallen her seven brothers." Then she was much troubled, and went to her father and mother and asked if it was true that she had had brothers, and what had become of them? The parents now dared keep the secret no longer, but said that what had befallen her brothers was the will of heaven and that her birth had only been the innocent cause.

But the maiden took it to heart daily, and thought she must deliver her brothers. She had no rest or peace until she set out secretly, and went forth into the wide world to trace out her brothers and set them free, let it cost what it might. She took nothing with her but a little ring belonging to her parents as a keepsake, a loaf of bread against hunger, a little pitcher of water against thirst, and a little chair as a provision against weariness.

And now she went continually onwards, far, far to the very end of the world. Then she came to the sun, but it was too hot and terrible and devoured little children. Hastily she ran away, and ran to the moon, but it was far too cold and also awful and malicious; and when it saw the child, it said, "I smell, I smell the flesh of men."

On this she ran swiftly away and came to the stars, which were kind and good to her, and each of them sat on its own particular little chair. But the morning star arose, and gave her the drumstick of a chicken, and said, "If thou hast not that drumstick, thou canst not open the glass mountain, and in the glass mountain are thy brothers."

The maiden took the drumstick, wrapped it carefully in a cloth, and went onwards again until she came to the glass mountain. The door was shut, and she thought she would take out the drumstick; but when she undid the cloth, it was empty, and she had lost the good star's present. What was she now to do? She wished to rescue her brothers and had no key to the glass mountain. The good sister took a knife, cut off one of her little fingers, put it in the door, and succeeded in opening it. When she had gone inside, a little dwarf came to meet her, who said, "My child, what are you looking for?"

"I am looking for my brothers, the seven ravens," she replied.

The dwarf said, "The lord ravens are not at home, but if you will wait here until they come, step in." Thereupon the little dwarf carried the ravens' dinner in, on seven little plates and in seven little glasses, and the little sister ate a morsel from each plate, and from each little glass she took a sip; but in the last little glass she dropped the ring which she had brought away with her.

Suddenly she heard a whirring of wings and a rushing through the air, and then the little dwarf said, "Now the lord ravens are flying home."

Then they came, and wanted to eat and drink, and looked for their little plates and glasses. Then said one after the other, "Who has eaten something from my plate? Who has drunk out of my little glass? It was a human mouth."

And when the seventh came to the bottom of the glass, the ring rolled against his mouth. Then he looked at it and saw that it was a ring belonging to

his father and mother, and said, "God grant that our sister may be here, and then we shall be free."

When the maiden, who was standing behind the door, watching, heard that wish, she came forth, and on this all the ravens were restored to their human form again. And they embraced and kissed one another, and went joyfully home.

# The Riddle

HERE WAS ONCE A KING'S SONG WHO WAS SEIZED with a desire to travel about the world, and took no one with him but a faithful servant. One day he came to a great forest; and when darkness overtook him, he could find no shelter and knew not where to pass the night. Then he saw a girl who was going towards a small house; and when he came nearer, he saw that the maiden was young and beautiful. He spoke to her, and said, "Dear child, can I and my servant find shelter for the night in the little house?"

"Oh, yes," said the girl in a sad voice, "that you certainly can, but I do not advise you to venture it. Do not go in."

"Why not?" asked the king's son.

The maiden sighed and said, "My stepmother practices wicked arts; she is ill-disposed toward strangers." Then he saw very well that he had come to the house of a witch, but as it was dark, and he could not go farther, and also was not afraid, he entered.

The old woman was sitting in an armchair by the fire and looked at the stranger with her red eyes. "Good evening," growled she, and pretended to be quite friendly. "Take a seat and rest yourselves." She blew up the fire on which she was cooking something in a small pot. The daughter warned the two to be prudent, to eat nothing and drink nothing, for the old woman brewed evil drinks.

They slept quietly until early morning. When they were making ready for their departure, and the king's son was already seated on his horse, the old woman said, "Stop a moment. I will first hand you a parting draught." Whilst she fetched it, the king's son rode away, and the servant, who had to buckle his saddle tight, was the only one present when the wicked witch came with the drink. "Take that to your master," said she. But at that instant the glass broke and the poison spurted on the horse; and it was so strong that the animal immediately fell down dead.

The servant ran after his master and told him what had happened, but would not leave his saddle behind him and ran back to fetch it. When, however, he came to the dead horse, a raven was already sitting on it, devouring it. "Who knows whether we shall find anything better today?" said the servant; so he killed the raven and took it with him. And now they journeyed onwards into the forest the whole day, but could not get out of it. By nightfall they found an inn and entered it. The servant gave the raven to the innkeeper to make ready for supper. They had, however, stumbled on a den of murderers; and during the darkness twelve of these came, intending to kill the strangers

and rob them. Before they set about this work, they sat down to supper, and the innkeeper and the witch sat down with them, and together they ate a dish of soup in which was cut up the flesh of the raven. Hardly, however, had they swallowed a couple of mouthfuls, before they all fell down dead, for the raven had communicated to them the poison from the horseflesh. There was no one else left in the house but the innkeeper's daughter, who was honest and had taken no part in their godless deeds. She opened all doors to the stranger and showed him the heaped-up treasures. But the king's son said she might keep everything; he would have none of it, and rode onwards with his servant.

After they had traveled about for a long time, they came to a town in which was a beautiful but proud princess, who had caused it to be proclaimed that whosoever should set her a riddle which she could not guess, that man should be her husband; but if she guessed it, his head must be cut off. She had three days to guess it in, but was so clever that she always found the answer to the riddle given her before the appointed time. Nine suitors had already perished in this manner, when the king's son arrived and, blinded by her great beauty, was willing to stake his life for it. Then he went to her and laid his riddle before her. "What is this?" said he. "One slew none, and yet slew twelve."

She did not know what that was; she thought and thought, but she could not find out; she opened her riddle books, but it was not in them—in short, her wisdom was at an end. As she did not know how to help herself, she ordered her maid to creep into the lord's sleeping chamber and listen to his dreams, and thought that he would perhaps speak in his sleep and discover the riddle. But the clever servant had placed himself in the bed instead of his master, and when the maid came there, he tore off from her the mantle in which she had wrapped herself, and chased her out with rods. The second night the king's daughter sent her maid-in-waiting, who was to see if she could succeed better in listening, but the servant took her mantle also away from her, and hunted her out with rods. Now the master believed himself safe for the third night, and lay down in his own bed. Then came the princess herself, and she had put on a misty-grey mantle, and she seated herself near him. And when she thought that he was asleep and dreaming, she spoke to him, and hoped that he would answer in his sleep, as many do, but he was awake and understood and heard everything quite well. Then she asked, "One slew none—what is that?"

He replied, "A raven, which ate of a dead and poisoned horse, and died of it."

She inquired further, "And yet slew twelve—what is that?"

He answered, "That means twelve murderers, who ate the raven and died of it."

When she knew the answer to the riddle, she wanted to steal away, but he held her mantle so fast that she was forced to leave it behind her.

Next morning, the king's daughter announced that she had guessed the riddle, and sent for the twelve judges and expounded it before them. But the youth begged for a hearing, and said, "She stole into my room in the night and questioned me; otherwise she could not have discovered it."

The judges said, "Bring us a proof of this." Then were the three mantles brought thither by the servant; and when the judges saw the misty-grey one which the king's daughter usually wore, they said, "Let the mantle be embroidered with gold and silver, and then it will be your wedding mantle."

# The Bremen Town Musicians

CERTAIN MAN HAD A DONKEY, WHICH HAD CARRIED the corn sacks to the mill indefatigably for many a long year; but his strength was going, and he was growing more and more unfit for work. Then his master began to consider how he might best save his keep; but the donkey, seeing that no good wind was blowing, ran away and set out on the road to Bremen. "There," he thought, "I can surely be town musician." When he had walked some distance, he found a hound lying on the road, gasping like one who had run till he was tired. "What are you gasping so for, you big fellow?" asked the donkey.

"Ah," replied the hound, "as I am old and daily grow weaker and no longer can hunt, my master wanted to kill me, so I took to flight; but now how am I to earn my bread?"

"I tell you what," said the donkey. "I am going to Bremen, and shall be town musician there; go with me and engage yourself also as a musician. I will play the lute, and you shall beat the kettledrum."

The hound agreed, and on they went.

Before long they came to a cat, sitting on the path, with a face like three rainy days! "Now then, old shaver, what has gone askew with you?" asked the donkey.

"Who can be merry when his neck is in danger?" answered the cat. "Because I am now getting old, and my teeth are worn to stumps, and I prefer to sit by the fire and spin, rather than hunt about after mice, my mistress wanted to drown me, so I ran away. But now good advice is scarce. Where am I to go?"

"Go with us to Bremen. You understand night music; you can be a town musician."

The cat thought well of it, and went with them. After this the three fugitives came to a farm-yard, where the cock was sitting upon the gate, crowing with all his might. "Your crow goes through and through one," said the donkey. "What is the matter?"

"I have been foretelling fine weather, because it is the day on which Our Lady washes the Christ child's little shirts and wants to dry them," said the cock; "but guests are coming for Sunday, so the housewife has no pity, and has told the cook that she intends to eat me in the soup tomorrow, and this evening I am to have my head cut off. Now I am crowing at full pitch while I can."

"Ah, but, red-comb," said the donkey, "you had better come away with us. We are going to Bremen. You can find something better than death everywhere: you have a good voice, and if we make music together, it must have some quality!"

The cock agreed to this plan, and all four went on together. They could not, however, reach the city of Bremen in one day; and in the evening they came to a forest where they meant to pass the night. The donkey and the hound lay themselves down under a large tree, the cat and the cock settled themselves in the branches; but the cock flew right to the top, where he was most safe. Before he went to sleep he looked round on all four sides and thought he saw in the distance a little spark burning; so he called out to his companions that there must be a house not far off, for he saw a light. The donkey said, "If so, we had better get up and go on, for the shelter here is bad." The hound thought that a few bones with some meat on would do him good, too!

So they made their way to the place where the light was; and soon saw it shine brighter and grow larger, until they came to a well-lighted robber's house. The donkey, as the biggest, went to the window and looked in.

"What do you see, my grey horse?" asked the cock.

"What do I see?" answered the donkey. "A table covered with good things to eat and drink, and robbers sitting at it, enjoying themselves."

"That would be the sort of thing for us," said the cock.

"Yes, yes; ah, how I wish we were there!" said the donkey.

Then the animals took counsel together how they should manage to drive away the robbers, and at last they thought of a plan. The donkey was to place himself with his forefeet upon the window ledge, the hound was to jump on the donkey's back, the cat was to climb upon the dog, and lastly the cock was to fly up and perch upon the head of the cat.

When this was done, at a given signal, they began to perform their music together: the donkey brayed, the hound barked, the cat mewed, and the cock crowed; then they burst through the window into the room, so that the glass clattered! At this horrible din, the robbers sprang up, thinking no otherwise than that a ghost had come in, and fled in a great fright out into the forest. The four companions now sat down at the table, well content with what was left, and ate as if they were going to fast for a month.

As soon as the four minstrels had done, they put out the light, and each sought for himself a sleeping place according to his nature and to what suited him. The donkey lay himself down upon some straw in the yard, the hound behind the door, the cat upon the hearth near the warm ashes, and the cock perched himself upon a beam of the roof; and being tired from their long walk, they soon went to sleep.

When it was past midnight, and the robbers saw from afar that the light was no longer burning in their house, and all appeared quiet, the captain said, "We ought not to have let ourselves be frightened out of our wits" and ordered one of them to go and examine the house.

The messenger, finding all still, went into the kitchen to light a candle, and, taking the glistening fiery eyes of the cat for live coals, he held a lucifer match to them to light it. But the cat did not understand the joke and flew in his face, spitting and scratching. He was dreadfully frightened and ran to the back door, but the dog who lay there sprang up and bit his leg; and as he ran across the yard by the straw heap, the donkey gave him a smart kick with its hind foot. The cock, too, who had been awakened by the noise, and had become lively, cried down from the beam, "Cock-a-doodle-doo!"

Then the robber ran back as fast as he could to his captain, and said, "Ah, there is a horrible witch sitting in the house, who spat on me and scratched my face with her long claws; and by the door stands a man with a knife, who stabbed me in the leg; and in the yard there lies a black monster, who beat me with a wooden club; and above, upon the roof, sits the judge, who called out, 'Bring the rogue here to me!' so I got away as well as I could."

After this the robbers did not trust themselves in the house again; but it suited the four musicians of Bremen so well that they did not care to leave it anymore. And the mouth of him who last told this story is still warm.

# The Singing Bone

N A CERTAIN COUNTRY THERE WAS ONCE GREAT lamentation over a wild boar that laid waste the farmer's fields, killed the cattle, and ripped up people's bodies with his tusks. The king promised a large reward to anyone who would free the land from this plague; but the beast was so big and strong that no one dared to go near the forest in which it lived. At last the king gave notice that whosoever should capture or kill the wild boar should have his only daughter to wife.

Now there lived in the country two brothers, sons of a poor man, who declared themselves willing to undertake the hazardous enterprise; the elder, who was crafty and shrewd, out of pride; the younger, who was innocent and simple, from a kind heart. The king said, "In order that you may be the more sure of finding the beast, you must go into the forest from opposite sides." So

the elder went in on the west side, and the younger on the east.

When the younger had gone a short way, a little man stepped up to him. He held in his hand a black spear and said, "I give you this spear because your heart is pure and good; with this you can boldly attack the wild boar, and it will do you no harm."

He thanked the little man, shouldered the spear, and went on fearlessly.

Before long he saw the beast, which rushed at him, but he held the spear towards it; and in its blind fury it ran so swiftly against it that its heart was cloven in twain. Then he took the monster on his back and went homewards with it to the king.

As he came out at the other side of the wood, there stood at the entrance a house where people were making merry with wine and dancing. His elder brother had gone in here, and, thinking that, after all, the boar would not run away from him, was going to drink until he felt brave. But when he saw his young brother coming out of the wood laden with his booty, his envious, evil heart gave him no peace. He called out to him, "Come in, dear brother; rest and refresh yourself with a cup of wine."

The youth, who suspected no evil, went in and told him about the good little man who had given him the spear wherewith he had slain the boar.

The elder brother kept him there until the evening, and then they went away together. And when in the darkness they came to a bridge over a brook, the elder brother let the other go first; and when he was halfway across, he gave him such a blow from behind that he fell down dead. He buried him beneath the bridge, took the boar, and carried it to the king, pretending that he had killed it; whereupon he obtained the king's daughter in marriage. And when his younger brother did not come back, he said, "The boar must have killed him," and everyone believed it.

But as nothing remains hidden from God, so this black deed also was to come to light.

Years afterwards a shepherd was driving his herd across the bridge, and saw lying in the sand beneath, a snow-white little bone. He thought that it

would make a good mouthpiece, so he clambered down, picked it up, and cut out of it a mouthpiece for his horn. But when he blew through it for the first time, to his great astonishment, the bone began of its own accord to sing:

*"Ah, friend, thou blowest upon my bone!*
*Long have I lain beside the water;*
*My brother slew me for the boar,*
*And took for his wife the king's young daughter."*

"What a wonderful horn!" said the shepherd. "It sings by itself; I must take it to my lord the king." And when he came with it to the king, the horn again began to sing its little song. The king understood it all and caused the ground below the bridge to be dug up; and then the whole skeleton of the murdered man came to light. The wicked brother could not deny the deed, and was sewn up in a sack and drowned. But the bones of the murdered man were laid to rest in a beautiful tomb in the churchyard.

# The Valiant Little Tailor

NE SUMMER'S MORNING A LITTLE TAILOR WAS sitting on his table by the window; he was in good spirits, and sewed with all his might. Then came a peasant woman down the street crying, "Good jams, cheap! Good jams, cheap!"

This rang pleasantly in the tailor's ears; he stretched his delicate head out of the window, and called, "Come up here, dear woman; here you will get rid of your goods." The woman came up the three steps to the tailor with her heavy basket, and he made her unpack the whole of the pots for him. He inspected all of them, lifted them up, put his nose to them, and at length said, "The jam seems to me to be good, so weigh me out four ounces, dear woman; and if it is a quarter of a pound that is of no consequence." The woman, who had hoped to find a good sale, gave him what he desired but went away quite angry and grumbling. "Now, God bless the jam to my use," cried the little tailor, "and give me health and strength"; so he brought the bread out of the cupboard, cut himself a piece right across the loaf, and spread the jam over it. "This won't taste bitter," said he, "but I will just finish the jacket before I take a bite." He laid the bread near him, sewed on, and in his joy, made bigger and bigger stitches. In the meantime the smell of the sweet jam ascended so to the wall to where the flies were sitting in great numbers and they were attracted and descended on it in hosts. "Hey! Who invited you?" said the little tailor, and drove the unbidden guests away. The flies, however, who understood no German, would not be turned away, but came back again in ever-increasing companies. The little tailor at last lost all patience and got a bit of cloth from the hole under his work-table, saying, "Wait, and I will give it to you," struck it mercilessly on them. When he drew it away and counted, there lay before him no fewer than seven, dead and with legs stretched out. "Art thou a fellow of that sort?" said he, and could not help admiring his own bravery. "The whole town shall know of this!" And the little tailor hastened to cut himself a girdle, stitched it, and embroidered on it in large letters *Seven at one stroke*! "What, the town!" he continued. "The whole world shall hear of it!" And his heart wagged with joy like a lamb's tail. The tailor put on the girdle, and resolved to go forth into the world, because he thought his workshop was too small for his valor. Before he went away, he sought about in the house to see if there was anything which he could take with him; however, he found nothing but an old cheese, and that he put in his pocket. In front of the door he observed a bird which had caught itself in the thicket. It had to go into his pocket with the cheese. Now he took to the road boldly, and as he was light and nimble, he felt no fatigue. The road led him up a mountain, and when he had

reached the highest point of it, there sat a powerful giant looking about him quite comfortably. The little tailor went bravely up, spoke to him, and said, "Good day, comrade; so thou art sitting there overlooking the widespread world! I am just on my way thither and want to try my luck. Hast thou any inclination to go with me?"

The giant looked contemptuously at the tailor and said, "Thou ragamuffin! Thou miserable creature!"

"Oh, indeed?" answered the little tailor, and unbuttoned his coat and showed the giant the girdle. "There mayest thou read what kind of a man I am!"

The giant read, "Seven at one stroke," and thought that they had been men whom the tailor had killed, and began to feel a little respect for the tiny fellow. Nevertheless, he wished to try him first, and took a stone in his hand

and squeezed it together so that water dropped out of it. "Do that likewise," said the giant, "if thou hast strength."

"Is that all?" said the tailor. "That is child's play with us!" And put his hand into his pocket, brought out the soft cheese, and pressed it until the liquid ran out of it. "Faith," said he, "that was a little better, wasn't it?"

The giant did not know what to say, and could not believe it of the little man. Then the giant picked up a stone and threw it so high that the eye could scarcely follow it. "Now, little mite of a man, do that likewise."

"Well thrown," said the tailor, "but after all the stone came down to earth again; I will throw you one which shall never come back at all." And he put his hand into his pocket, took out the bird, and threw it into the air. The bird, delighted with its liberty, rose, flew away, and did not come back. "How does that shot please you, comrade?" asked the tailor.

"Thou canst certainly throw," said the giant, "but now we will see if thou art able to carry anything properly." He took the little tailor to a mighty oak tree, which lay there felled on the ground, and said, "If thou art strong enough, help me to carry the tree out of the forest."

"Readily," answered the little man; "take thou the trunk on thy shoulders, and I will raise up the branches and twigs; after all, they are the heaviest." The giant took the trunk on his shoulder, but the tailor seated himself on a branch, and the giant, who could not look round, had to carry away the whole tree, and the little tailor into the bargain: he, behind, was quite merry and happy, and whistled the song "Three tailors rode forth from the gate," as if carrying the tree were child's play.

The giant, after he had dragged the heavy burden part of the way, could go no farther, and cried, "Hark you, I shall have to let the tree fall!" The tailor sprang nimbly down, seized the tree with both arms as if he had been carrying it, and said to the giant, "Thou art such a great fellow and yet canst not even carry the tree!"

They went on together, and as they passed a cherry tree, the giant laid hold of the top of the tree where the ripest fruit was hanging, bent it down, gave it into the tailor's hand, and bade him eat. But the little tailor was much too weak to hold the tree; and when the giant let it go, it sprang back again, and the tailor was hurried into the air with it. When he had fallen down again without injury, the giant said, "What is this? Hast thou not strength enough to hold the weak twig?"

"There is no lack of strength," answered the little tailor. "Dost thou think that could be anything to a man who has struck down seven at one blow? I leapt over the tree because the huntsmen are shooting down there in the thicket. Jump as I did, if thou canst do it." The giant made the attempt, but could not get over the tree and remained hanging in the branches, so that in this also the tailor kept the upper hand.

The giant said, "If thou art such a valiant fellow, come with me into our cavern and spend the night with us." The little tailor was willing, and followed him. When they went into the cave, other giants were sitting there by the fire, and each of them had a roasted sheep in his hand and was eating it.

The little tailor looked round and thought, "It is much more spacious here than in my workshop." The giant showed him a bed, and said he was to lie down in it and sleep. The bed, however, was too big for the little tailor; he did not lie down in it but crept into a corner. When it was midnight, and the giant thought that the little tailor was lying in a sound sleep, he got up, took a great iron bar, cut through the bed with one blow, and thought he had given

the grasshopper his finishing stroke. With the earliest dawn the giants went into the forest, and had quite forgotten the little tailor, when all at once he walked up to them quite merrily and boldly. The giants were terrified; they were afraid that he would strike them all dead, and ran away in a great hurry.

The little tailor went onwards, always following his own pointed nose. After he had walked for a long time, he came to the courtyard of a royal palace, and as he felt weary, he lay down on the grass and fell asleep. Whilst he lay there, the people came and inspected him on all sides, and read on his girdle, *Seven at one stroke*. "Ah," said they, "what does the great warrior here in the midst of peace? He must be a mighty lord." They went and announced him to the king and gave it as their opinion that if war should break out, this would be a weighty and useful man who ought on no account to be allowed to depart. The counsel pleased the king, and he sent one of his courtiers to the little tailor to offer him military service when he awoke. The ambassador remained standing by the sleeper, waited until he stretched his limbs and opened his eyes, and then conveyed to him this proposal.

"For this very reason have I come here," the tailor replied. "I am ready to enter the king's service." He was therefore honorably received and a special dwelling was assigned him.

The soldiers, however, were set against the little tailor, and wished him a thousand miles away. "What is to be the end of this?" they said amongst themselves. "If we quarrel with him, and he strikes about him, seven of us will fall at every blow; not one of us can stand against him." They came therefore to a decision, betook themselves in a body to the king, and begged for their dismissal. "We are not prepared," said they, "to stay with a man who kills seven at one stroke." The king was sorry that for the sake of one he should lose all his faithful servants, wished that he had never set eyes on the tailor, and would willingly have been rid of him again. But he did not venture to give him his dismissal, for he dreaded lest he should strike him and all his people dead and place himself on the royal throne. He thought about it for a long time, and at last found good counsel. He sent to the little tailor and caused him to be informed that as he was such a great warrior, he had one request to make to him. In a forest of his country lived two giants who caused great mischief with their robbing, murdering, ravaging, and burning; and no one could approach them without putting himself in danger of death. If the tailor conquered and killed these two giants, he would give him his only daughter to wife and half of his kingdom as a dowry, likewise one hundred horsemen should go with him to assist him.

"That would indeed be a fine thing for a man like me!" thought the little tailor. "One is not offered a beautiful princess and half a kingdom every day of one's life!"

"Oh, yes," he replied, "I will soon subdue the giants, and do not require the help of the hundred horsemen to do it; he who can hit seven with one blow has no need to be afraid of two."

The little tailor went forth, and the hundred horsemen followed him. When he came to the outskirts of the forest, he said to his followers, "Just stay waiting here. I alone will soon finish off the giants." Then he bounded into the forest and looked about right and left. After a while he perceived both giants. They lay sleeping under a tree, and snored so that the branches waved up and down. The little tailor, not idle, gathered two pocketfuls of stones, and with these climbed up the tree. When he was halfway up, he slipped down by a branch, until he sat just above the sleepers, and then let one stone after another fall on the breast of one of the giants.

For a long time the giant felt nothing, but at last he awoke, pushed his comrade, and said, "Why art thou knocking me?"

"Thou must be dreaming," said the other. "I am not knocking thee." They laid themselves down to sleep again, and then the tailor threw a stone down on the second. "What is the meaning of this?" cried the other. "Why art thou pelting me?"

"I am not pelting thee," answered the first, growling. They disputed about it for a time, but as they were weary they let the matter rest, and their eyes closed once more. The little tailor began his game again, picked out the biggest stone, and threw it with all his might on the breast of the first giant. "That is too bad!" cried he, and sprang up like a madman and pushed his companion against the tree until it shook. The other paid him back in the same coin, and they got into such a rage that they tore up trees and belabored each other so

long, that at last they both fell down dead on the ground at the same time.

Then the little tailor leapt down. "It is a lucky thing," said he, "that they did not tear up the tree on which I was sitting, or I should have had to spring onto another like a squirrel; but we tailors are nimble." He drew out his sword and gave each of them a couple of thrusts in the breast, and then went out to the horsemen and said, "The work is done; I have given both of them their finishing stroke, but it was hard work! They tore up trees in their sore need, and defended themselves with them, but all that is to no purpose when a man like myself comes, who can kill seven at one blow."

"But are you not wounded?" asked the horsemen.

"You need not concern yourself about that," answered the tailor. "They have not bent one hair of mine." The horsemen would not believe him, and rode into the forest; there they found the giants swimming in their blood, and all round about lay the torn-up trees.

The little tailor demanded of the king the promised reward; he, however, repented of his promise, and again bethought himself how he could get rid of the hero. "Before thou receivest my daughter and the half of my kingdom," said he to him, "thou must perform one more heroic deed. In the forest roams a unicorn which does great harm, and thou must catch it first."

"I fear one unicorn still less than two giants. Seven at one blow is my kind of affair." He took a rope and an axe with him, went forth into the forest, and again bade those who were sent with him to wait outside. He had not long to seek. The unicorn soon came towards him and rushed directly on the tailor, as if it would spit him on his horn without more ceremony. "Softly, softly; it can't be done as quickly as that," said he, and stood still and waited until the animal was quite close, and then sprang nimbly behind the tree. The unicorn

SEVEN
AT ONE
STROKE

ran against the tree with all its strength, and struck its horn so fast in the trunk that it had not strength enough to draw it out again, and thus it was caught. "Now, I have got the bird," said the tailor, and came out from behind the tree and put the rope round its neck, and then with his axe he hewed the horn out of the tree, and when all was ready he led the beast away and took it to the king.

The king still would not give him the promised reward, and made a third demand. Before the wedding the tailor was to catch him a wild boar that made great havoc in the forest, and the huntsmen should give him their help. "Willingly," said the tailor, "that is child's play!" He did not take the huntsmen with him into the forest, and they were well pleased that he did not, for the wild boar had several times received them in such a manner that they had no inclination to lie in wait for him. When the boar perceived the tailor, it ran on him with foaming mouth and whetted tusks, and was about to throw him to the ground, but the active hero sprang into a chapel which was near, and up to the window at once, and in one bound out again. The boar ran in after him, but the tailor ran round outside and shut the door behind it, and then the raging beast, which was much too heavy and awkward to leap out of the window, was caught. The little tailor called the huntsmen thither that they might see the prisoner with their own eyes. The hero, however went to the king, who was now, whether he liked it or not, obliged to keep his promise, and gave him his daughter and the half of his kingdom. Had he known that it was no warlike hero, but a little tailor who was standing before him, it would have gone to his heart still more than it did. The wedding was held with great magnificence and small joy, and out of a tailor a king was made.

After some time the young queen heard her husband say in his dreams at night, "Boy, make me the doublet and patch the pantaloons, or else I will rap the yard-measure over thine ears." Then she discovered in what state of life the young lord had been born, and next morning complained of her wrongs to her father and begged him to help her to get rid of her husband, who was nothing else but a tailor.

The king comforted her and said, "Leave thy bedroom door open this night, and my servants shall stand outside; and when he has fallen asleep shall go in, bind him, and take him on board a ship which shall carry him into the wide world." The woman was satisfied with this; but the king's armor-bearer, who had heard all, was friendly with the young lord and informed him of the whole plot.

"I'll put a screw into that business," said the little tailor. At night he went to bed with his wife at the usual time, and when she thought that he had fallen asleep, she got up, opened the door, and then lay down again. The little tailor, who was only pretending to be asleep, began to cry out in a clear voice, "Boy, make me the doublet and patch me the pantaloons, or I will rap the yard-measure over thine ears. I smote seven at one blow. I killed two giants, I brought away one unicorn and caught a wild boar, and am I to fear those who are standing outside the room." When these men heard the tailor speaking thus, they were overcome by a great dread and ran as if the Wild Huntsman were behind them, and none of them would venture anything further against him. So the little tailor was a king and remained one to the end of his life.

# The Tailor in Heaven

NE VERY FINE DAY IT CAME TO PASS THAT THE good God wished to enjoy himself in the heavenly garden and took all the apostles and saints with him, so that no one stayed in heaven but Saint Peter. The Lord had commanded him to let no one in during his absence, so Peter stood by the door and kept watch.

Before long someone knocked. Peter asked who was there and what he wanted. "I am a poor, honest tailor who prays for admission," replied a smooth voice.

"Honest indeed," said Peter, "like the thief on the gallows! Thou hast been light-fingered and hast snipped folks' clothes away. Thou wilt not get into heaven. The Lord hath forbidden me to let anyone in while he is out."

"Come, do be merciful," cried the tailor. "Little scraps which fall off the table of their own accord are not stolen and are not worth speaking about. Look, I am lame and have blisters on my feet with walking here; I cannot possibly turn back again. Only let me in, and I will do all the rough work. I will carry the children and wash their clothes, and wash and clean the benches on which they have been playing, and patch all their torn clothes."

Saint Peter let himself be moved by pity and opened the door of heaven just wide enough for the lame tailor to slip his lean body in. He was forced to sit down in a corner behind the door, and was to stay quietly and peaceably there, in order that the Lord, when he returned, might not observe him and be angry. The tailor obeyed, but once when Saint Peter went outside the door, he got up, and full of curiosity, went round about into every corner of heaven, and inspected the arrangement of every place. At length he came to a spot where many beautiful and delightful chairs were standing, and in the midst was a seat all of gold which was set with shining jewels; likewise it was much higher than the other chairs, and a footstool of gold was before it. It was, however, the seat on which the Lord sat when he was at home and from which he could see everything which happened on earth. The tailor stood still, and looked at the seat for a long time, for it pleased him better than all else. At last he could master his curiosity no longer, and climbed up and seated himself in the chair. Then he saw everything which was happening on earth, and observed an ugly old woman who was standing washing by the side of a stream, secretly laying two veils on one side for herself. The sight of this made the tailor so angry that he laid hold of the golden footstool, and threw it down to earth through heaven, at the old thief. As, however, he could not bring the stool back again, he slipped quietly out of the chair, seated himself in his place behind the door, and behaved as if he had never stirred from the spot.

When the lord and master came back again with his heavenly companions, he did not see the tailor behind the door, but when he seated himself on his chair, the footstool was missing. He asked Saint Peter what had become of the stool, but he did not know. Then he asked if he had let anyone come in. "I know of no one who has been here," answered Peter, "but a lame tailor, who is still sitting behind the door."

Then the Lord had the tailor brought before him and asked him if he had taken away the stool and where he had put it.

"Oh, Lord," answered the tailor joyously, "I threw it in my anger down to earth at an old woman whom I saw stealing two veils at the washing."

"Oh, thou knave," said the Lord, "were I to judge as thou judgest, how dost thou think thou couldst have escaped so long? I should long ago have had no chairs, benches, seats—nay, not even an oven-fork—but should have thrown everything down at the sinners. Henceforth thou canst stay no longer in heaven but must go outside the door again. Then go where thou wilt. No one shall give punishment here, but I alone, the Lord."

Peter was obliged to take the tailor out of heaven again, and as he had torn shoes and feet covered with blisters, he took a stick in his hand and went to Wait-a-Bit, where the good soldiers sit and make merry.

# The Louse and the Flea

LOUSE AND A FLEA KEPT HOUSE TOGETHER AND were brewing beer in an eggshell. Then the little louse fell in and burnt herself. On this the little flea began to scream loudly. Then said the little room-door, "Little flea, why art thou screaming?"

"Because the louse has burnt herself."

Then the little door began to creak. On this, a little broom in the corner said, "Why art thou creaking, little door?"

"Have I not reason to creak?

*The little louse has burnt herself,*

*The little flea is weeping.*"

So the little broom began to sweep frantically. Then a little cart passed by and said, "Why art thou sweeping, little broom?"

"Have I not reason to sweep?

*The little louse has burnt herself,*

*The little flea is weeping,*

*The little door is creaking."*

So the little cart said, "Then I will run," and began to run wildly.

Then said the ash-heap by which it ran, "Why art thou running so, little cart?"

"Have I not reason to run?

*The little louse has burnt herself,*

*The little flea is weeping,*

*The little door is creaking,*

*The little broom is sweeping."*

The ash-heap said, "Then I will burn furiously," and began to burn in clear flames.

A little tree stood near the ash-heap and said, "Ash-heap, why art thou burning?"

"Have I not reason to burn?

*The little louse has burnt herself,*

*The little flea is weeping,*

*The little door is creaking,*

*The little broom is sweeping,*

*The little cart is running."*

The little tree said, "Then I will shake myself," and began to shake herself so that all her leaves fell off.

A girl who came up with her water-pitcher saw that, and said, "Little tree, why art thou shaking thyself?"

"Have I not reason to shake myself?

*The little louse has burnt herself,*

*The little flea is weeping,*

*The little door is creaking,*

*The little broom is sweeping,*

*The little cart is running,*

*The little ash-heap is burning.*"

On this the girl said, "Then I will break my little water pitcher," and she broke her little water-pitcher.

Then said the little spring from which ran the water, "Girl, why art thou breaking thy water-jug?"

"Have I not reason to break my water-jug?

*The little louse has burnt herself,*

*The little flea is weeping,*

*The little door is creaking,*

*The little broom is sweeping,*

*The little cart is running,*

*The little ash-heap is burning,*

*The little tree is shaking itself."*

"Oh, ho!" said the spring, "then I will begin to flow," and began to flow violently. And in the water everything was drowned, the girl, the little tree, the little ash-heap, the little cart, the broom, the little door, the little flea, the little louse, all together.

# The Girl Without Hands

CERTAIN MILLER HAD LITTLE BY LITTLE FALLEN into poverty and had nothing left but his mill and a large apple tree behind it. Once when he had gone into the forest to fetch wood, an old man stepped up to him, whom he had never seen before, and said, "Why dost thou plague thyself with cutting wood? I will make thee rich, if thou wilt promise me what is standing behind thy mill."

"What can that be but my apple tree?" thought the miller, and said, "yes," and gave a written promise to the stranger.

He, however, laughed mockingly and said, "When three years have passed, I will come and carry away what belongs to me," and then he went.

When the miller got home, his wife came to meet him and said, "Tell me, miller, from whence comes this sudden wealth into our house? All at once

every box and chest was filled; no one brought it in, and I know not how it happened."

He answered, "It comes from a stranger who met me in the forest and promised me great treasure. I, in return, have promised him what stands behind the mill; we can very well give him the big apple tree for it."

"Ah, Husband," said the terrified wife, "that must have been the devil! He did not mean the apple tree, but our daughter, who was standing behind the mill, sweeping the yard."

The miller's daughter was a beautiful, pious girl, and lived through the three years in the fear of God and without sin. When therefore the time was over, and the day came when the Evil One was to fetch her, she washed herself clean and made a circle round herself with chalk.

The devil appeared quite early, but he could not come near to her. Angrily, he said to the miller, "Take all water away from her, that she may no longer be able to wash herself, for otherwise I have no power over her." The miller was afraid, and did so. The next morning the devil came again, but she had wept on her hands, and they were quite clean.

Again he could not get near her, and furiously said to the miller, "Cut her hands off, or else I cannot get the better of her."

The miller was shocked and answered, "How could I cut off my own child's hands?"

Then the Evil One threatened him and said, "If thou dost not do it, thou art mine, and I will take thee thyself."

The father became alarmed and promised to obey him. So he went to the girl and said, "My child, if I do not cut off both thine hands, the devil will carry me away; and in my terror I have promised to do it. Help me in my need, and forgive me the harm I do thee."

She replied, "Dear father, do with me what you will. I am your child." Thereupon she laid down both her hands and let them be cut off. The devil came for the third time, but she had wept so long and so much on the stumps, that after all they were quite clean. Then he had to give in, and had lost all right over her.

The miller said to her, "I have by means of thee received such great wealth that I will keep thee most delicately as long as thou livest."

But she replied, "Here I cannot stay. I will go forth; compassionate people will give me as much as I require." Thereupon she caused her maimed arms to be bound to her back, and by sunrise she set out on her way, and walked the whole day until night fell. Then she came to a royal garden, and by the shimmering of the moon she saw that trees covered with beautiful fruits grew in it, but she could not enter, for there was much water round about it. And as she had walked the whole day and not eaten one mouthful, and hunger tormented her, she thought, "Ah, if I were but inside that I might eat of the fruit, else must I die of hunger!" Then she knelt down, called on God the

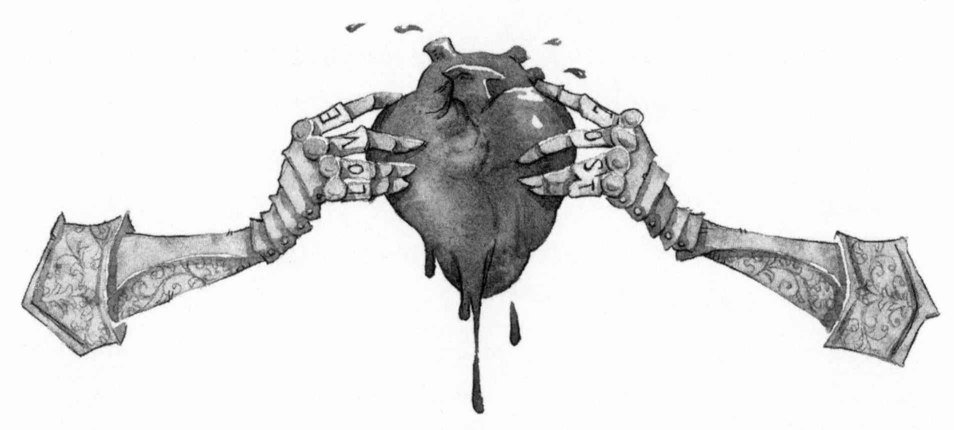


Lord, and prayed. And suddenly an angel came towards her who made a dam in the water, so that the moat became dry and she could walk through it. And now she went into the garden and the angel went with her. She saw a tree covered with beautiful pears, but they were all counted. Then she went to them, and to still her hunger, ate one with her mouth from the tree, but no more. The gardener was watching; but as the angel was standing by, he was afraid and thought the maiden was a spirit, and was silent; neither did he dare to cry out or to speak to the spirit. When she had eaten the pear, she was satisfied, and went and concealed herself among the bushes.

The king, to whom the garden belonged, came down to it next morning, and counted and saw that one of the pears was missing, and asked the gardener what had become of it, as it was not lying beneath the tree but was gone. Then answered the gardener, "Last night, a spirit came in, who had no hands, and ate off one of the pears with its mouth."

The king said, "How did the spirit get over the water, and where did it go after it had eaten the pear?"

The gardener answered, "Someone came in a snow-white garment from heaven who made a dam, and kept back the water, that the spirit might walk through the moat. And as it must have been an angel, I was afraid and asked no questions and did not cry out. When the spirit had eaten the pear, it went back again."

The king said, "If it be as thou sayest, I will watch with thee tonight."

When it grew dark, the king came into the garden and brought a priest with him, who was to speak to the spirit. All three seated themselves beneath the tree and watched. At midnight the maiden came creeping out of the thicket, went to the tree, and again ate one pear off it with her mouth; and beside her stood the angel in white garments.

Then the priest went out to them and said, "Comest thou from heaven or from earth? Art thou a spirit or a human being?"

She replied, "I am no spirit but an unhappy mortal deserted by all but God."

The king said, "If thou art forsaken by all the world, yet will I not forsake thee." He took her with him into his royal palace, and as she was so beautiful and good, he loved her with all his heart, had silver hands made for her, and took her to wife.

After a year the king had to take the field, so he commended his young queen to the care of his mother and said, "If she is brought to bed, take care of her, nurse her well, and tell me of it at once in a letter."

Then she gave birth to a fine boy. So the old mother made haste to write and announce the joyful news to him. But the messenger rested by a brook on the way, and as he was fatigued by the great distance, he fell asleep. Then came the devil, who was always seeking to injure the good queen, and exchanged the letter for another, in which was written that the queen had brought a monster into the world.

When the king read the letter, he was shocked and much troubled, but he wrote in answer that they were to take great care of the queen and nurse her well until his arrival. The messenger went back with the letter but rested at the same place and again fell asleep. Then came the devil once more and put a different letter in his pocket, in which it was written that they were to put the queen and her child to death.

The old mother was terribly shocked when she received the letter and could not believe it. She wrote back again to the king, but received no other answer, because each time the devil substituted a false letter; and in the last letter it was also written that she was to preserve the queen's tongue and eyes as a token that she had obeyed.

But the old mother wept to think such innocent blood was to be shed, and had a hind brought by night and cut out her tongue and eyes, and kept them. Then said she to the queen, "I cannot have thee killed as the king commands, but here thou mayest stay no longer. Go forth into the wide world with thy child, and never come here again."

The poor woman tied her child on her back, and went away with eyes full of tears. She came into a great wild forest, and then she fell on her knees and prayed to God; and the angel of the Lord appeared to her and led her to a little house on which was a sign with the words "Here all dwell free." A snow-white maiden came out of the little house and said, "Welcome, Lady Queen," and conducted her inside. Then they unbound the little boy from her back, and held him to her breast that he might feed, and laid him in a beautifully made little bed.

Then said the poor woman, "From whence knowest thou that I was a queen?"

The white maiden answered, "I am an angel sent by God, to watch over thee and thy child." The queen stayed seven years in the little house, and was

well cared for; and by God's grace, because of her piety, her hands that had been cut off grew once more.

At last the king came home again from the war, and his first wish was to see his wife and the child. Then his aged mother began to weep and said, "Thou wicked man, why didst thou write to me that I was to take those two innocent lives?" and she showed him the two letters the Evil One had forged, and then continued. "I did as thou badest me," and she showed the tokens, the tongue and eyes. Then the king began to weep for his poor wife and his little son so much more bitterly than she was doing that the aged mother had compassion on him and said, "Be at peace, she still lives; I secretly caused a hind to be killed and took these tokens from it; but I bound the child to thy wife's back and bade her go forth into the wide world, and made her promise never to come back here again, because thou wert so angry with her."

Then spoke the king, "I will go as far as the sky is blue, and will neither eat nor drink until I have found again my dear wife and my child, if in the meantime they have not been killed or died of hunger."

Thereupon the king traveled about for seven long years, and sought her in every cleft of the rocks and in every cave, but he found her not and thought she had died of want. During the whole of this time he neither ate nor drank, but God supported him.

At length he came into a great forest, and found therein the little house whose sign was "Here all dwell free." Then forth came the white maiden, took him by the hand, led him in, and said, "Welcome, Lord King," and asked him from whence he came.

He answered, "Soon shall I have traveled about for the space of seven years, and I seek my wife and her child, but cannot find them." The angel offered him meat and drink, but he did not take anything, and only wished to rest a little. Then he lay down to sleep, and put a handkerchief over his face.

Thereupon the angel went into the chamber where the queen sat with her son, whom she usually called Sorrowful, and said to her, "Go out with thy child; thy husband hath come." So she went to the place where he lay, and the handkerchief fell from his face. Then said she, "Sorrowful, pick up thy father's handkerchief and cover his face again." The child picked it up, and put it over his face again. The king in his sleep heard what passed, and had pleasure in letting the handkerchief fall once more.

But the child grew impatient, and said, "Dear Mother, how can I cover my father's face when I have no father in this world? I have learnt to say the prayer 'Our Father, which art in heaven'; thou hast told me that my father was in heaven and was the good God, and how can I know a wild man like this? He is not my father."

When the king heard that, he got up, and asked who they were. Then said she, "I am thy wife, and that is thy son, Sorrowful."

And he saw her living hands, and said, "My wife had silver hands."

She answered, "The good God has caused my natural hands to grow again"; and the angel went into the inner room and brought the silver hands and showed them to him. Hereupon he knew for a certainty that it was his dear wife and his dear child, and he kissed them and was glad, and said, "A heavy stone has fallen from off mine heart." Then the angel of God gave them one meal with her, and after that they went home to the king's aged mother. There were great rejoicings everywhere, and the king and queen were married again, and lived contentedly to their happy end.

# The Elves

## ~ First Story ~

SHOEMAKER, BY NO FAULT OF HIS OWN, HAD BECOME so poor that at last he had nothing left but leather for one pair of shoes. So in the evening, he cut out the shoes which he wished to begin to make the next morning, and as he had a good conscience, he lay down quietly in his bed, commended himself to God, and fell asleep. In the morning, after he had said his prayers, and was just going to sit down to work, the two shoes stood quite finished on his table. He was astounded, and knew not what to say to it. He took the shoes in his hands to observe them closer, and they were so neatly made that there was not one bad stitch in them, just as if they were intended as a masterpiece. Soon after, a buyer came in, and as the shoes pleased him so well, he paid more for them than was customary; and, with the money, the shoemaker was able to purchase leather for two pairs of shoes. He cut them out at night, and next morning was about to set to work with fresh courage; but he had no need to do so, for, when he got up, they were already made, and buyers also were not wanting who gave him money enough to buy leather for four pairs of shoes. The following morning, too, he found the four pairs made; and so it went on constantly, what he cut out in the evening was finished by the morning, so that he soon had his honest independence again, and at last became a wealthy man.

Now it befell that one evening not long before Christmas, when the man had been cutting out, he said to his wife, before going to bed, "What think you if we were to stay up tonight to see who it is that lends us this helping hand?" The woman liked the idea and lighted a candle, and then they hid themselves in a corner of the room, behind some clothes which were hanging up there, and watched. When it was midnight, two pretty little naked men came, sat down by the shoemaker's table, took all the work which was cut out before them and began to stitch and sew and hammer so skillfully and so quickly with their little fingers that the shoemaker could not turn away his eyes for astonishment. They did not stop until all was done and stood finished on the table, and they ran quickly away.

Next morning the woman said, "The little men have made us rich, and we really must show that we are grateful for it. They run about so, and have nothing on and must be cold. I'll tell thee what I'll do: I will make them little shirts and coats and vests and trousers, and knit both of them a pair of stockings, and do thou, too, make them two little pairs of shoes."

The man said, "I shall be very glad to do it"; and one night, when everything was ready, they laid their presents all together on the table instead of the cut-out work, and then concealed themselves to see how the little men

would behave. At midnight they came bounding in, and wanted to get to work at once, but as they did not find any leather cut out, but only the pretty little articles of clothing, they were at first astonished, and then they showed intense delight. They dressed themselves with the greatest rapidity, putting the pretty clothes on, and singing,

*"Now we are boys so fine to see,*
*Why should we longer cobblers be?"*

Then they danced and skipped and leapt over chairs and benches. At last they danced out of doors. From that time forth they came no more, but as long as the shoemaker lived all went well with him, and all his undertakings prospered.

## ~ Second Story ~

THERE WAS ONCE A POOR SERVANT GIRL, WHO WAS INDUSTRIOUS AND cleanly, and swept the house every day and emptied her sweepings on the great heap in front of the door. One morning when she was just going back to her work, she found a letter on this heap, and as she could not read, she put her broom in the corner and took the letter to her master and mistress; and behold it was an invitation from the elves, who asked the girl to hold a child for them at its christening. The girl did not know what to do, but at length, after much persuasion, and as they told her that it was not right to refuse an invitation of this kind, she consented.

Then three elves came and conducted her to a hollow mountain, where the little folks lived. Everything there was small but more elegant and beautiful than can be described. The baby's mother lay in a bed of black ebony ornamented with pearls; the coverlids were embroidered with gold; the cradle was of ivory, the bath of gold. The girl stood as godmother, and then wanted to go home again, but the little elves urgently entreated her to stay three days with them. So she stayed, and passed the time in pleasure and gaiety; and the little folks did all they could to make her happy. At last she set out on her way home. Then first they filled her pockets quite full of money, and after that they led her out of the mountain again. When she got home, she wanted to begin her work, and took the broom, which was still standing in the corner, in her hand and began to sweep. Then some strangers came out of the house who asked her who she was, and what business she had there. And she had not, as she thought, been three days with the little men in the mountains, but seven years, and in the meantime her former masters had died.

## ~ Third Story ~

A CERTAIN MOTHER'S CHILD HAD BEEN TAKEN AWAY OUT OF ITS CRADLE by the elves, and a changeling with a large head and staring eyes, which would do nothing but eat and drink, laid in its place. In her trouble she went to her neighbor and asked her advice. The neighbor said that she was to carry the changeling into the kitchen, set it down on the hearth, light a fire, and boil some water in two eggshells, which would make the changeling laugh, and if he laughed, all would be over with him.

The woman did everything that her neighbor bade her. When she put the eggshells with water on the fire, the imp said, "I am as old now as the Wester Forest, but never yet have I seen anyone boil anything in an eggshell!" And he began to laugh at it. Whilst he was laughing, suddenly came a host of little elves, who brought the right child, set it down on the hearth, and took the changeling away with them.

# Mother Holle

HERE WAS ONCE A WIDOW WHO HAD TWO daughters—one of whom was pretty and industrious, whilst the other was ugly and idle. But she was much fonder of the ugly and idle one, because she was her own daughter; and the other, who was a stepdaughter, was obliged to do all the work and be the Cinderella of the house. Every day the poor girl had to sit by a well in the highway and spin and spin till her fingers bled.

Now it happened that one day the shuttle was marked with her blood, so she dipped it in the well, to wash the mark off; but it dropped out of her hand and fell to the bottom. She began to weep, and ran to her stepmother and told her of the mishap. But she scolded her sharply and was so merciless as to say, "Since you have let the shuttle fall in, you must fetch it out again."

So the girl went back to the well, and did not know what to do; and in the sorrow of her heart she jumped into the well to get the shuttle. She lost her senses; and when she awoke and came to herself again, she was in a lovely meadow where the sun was shining and many thousands of flowers were growing. Along this meadow she went, and at last came to a baker's oven full of bread, and the bread cried out, "Oh, take me out! Take me out or I shall burn! I have been baked a long time!" So she went up to it and took out all the loaves one after another with the bread shovel. After that she went on till she came to a tree covered with apples, which called out to her, "Oh, shake me! Shake me! We apples are all ripe!" So she shook the tree till the apples fell like rain, and went on shaking till they were all down; and when she had gathered them into a heap, she went on her way.

At last she came to a little house, out of which an old woman peeped; but she had such large teeth that the girl was frightened and was about to run away. But the old woman called out to her, "What are you afraid of, dear child? Stay with me; if you will do all the work in the house properly, you shall be the better for it. Only you must take care to make my bed well and shake it thoroughly till the feathers fly—for then there is snow on the earth. I am Mother Holle."

As the old woman spoke so kindly to her, the girl took courage and agreed to enter her service. She attended to everything to the satisfaction of her mistress, and always shook her bed so vigorously that the feathers flew about like snow-flakes. So she had a pleasant life with her; never an angry word and boiled or roast meat every day.

She stayed some time with Mother Holle, and then she became sad. At first she did not know what was the matter with her but found at length that it was

home-sickness: although she was many thousand times better off here than at home, still she had a longing to be there. At last she said to the old woman, "I have a longing for home; and however well off I am down here, I cannot stay any longer. I must go up again to my own people."

Mother Holle said, "I am pleased that you long for your home again, and as you have served me so truly, I myself will take you up again." Thereupon she took her by the hand and led her to a large door. The door was opened, and just as the maiden was standing beneath the doorway, a heavy shower of golden rain fell, and all the gold remained sticking to her, so that she was completely covered over with it.

"You shall have that because you have been so industrious," said Mother Holle, and at the same time she gave her back the shuttle which she had let fall into the well. Thereupon the door closed, and the maiden found herself up above upon the earth, not far from her mother's house.

And as she went into the yard the cock was standing by the well side, and cried—

*"Cock-a-doodle-doo!*

*Your golden girl's come back to you!"*

So she went in to her mother; and as she arrived thus covered with gold, she was well received, both by her and her sister. The girl told all that had happened to her; and as soon as the mother heard how she had come by so much wealth, she was very anxious to obtain the same good luck for the ugly and lazy daughter. She had to seat herself by the well and spin; and in order that her shuttle might be stained with blood, she stuck her hand into a thornbush and pricked her finger. Then she threw her shuttle into the well and jumped in after it.

She came, like the other, to the beautiful meadow and walked along the very same path. When she got to the oven the bread again cried, "Oh, take me out! Take me out or I shall burn! I have been baked a long time!"

But the lazy thing answered, "As if I had any wish to make myself dirty," and on she went.

Soon she came to the apple tree, which cried, "Oh, shake me! Shake me! We apples are all ripe!"

But she answered, "I like that! One of you might fall on my head," and so went on.

When she came to Mother Holle's house, she was not afraid, for she had already heard of her big teeth, and she hired herself to her immediately.

The first day she forced herself to work diligently and obeyed Mother Holle when she told her to do anything, for she was thinking of all the gold that she would give her. But on the second day she began to be lazy, and on

the third day still more so; and then she would not get up in the morning at all. Neither did she make Mother Holle's bed as she ought, and did not shake it so as to make the feathers fly up. Mother Holle was soon tired of this and gave her notice to leave. The lazy girl was willing enough to go, and thought that now the golden rain would come. Mother Holle led her also to the great door; but while she was standing beneath it, instead of the gold a big kettleful of pitch was emptied over her. "That is the reward for your service," said Mother Holle, and shut the door.

So the lazy girl went home; but she was quite covered with pitch, and the cock by the well side, as soon as he saw her, cried out —

*"Cock-a-doodle-doo!*
*Your pitchy girl's come back to you!"*

But the pitch stuck fast to her, and could not be got off as long as she lived.

# Clever Elsie

HERE WAS ONCE A MAN WHO HAD A DAUGHTER WHO was called Clever Elsie. And when she had grown up, her father said, "We will get her married."

"Yes," said the mother, "if only anyone would come who would have her."

At length a man came from a distance and wooed her, who was called Hans; but he stipulated that Clever Elsie should be really wise. "Oh," said the father, "she's sharp enough."

And the mother said, "Oh, she can see the wind coming up the street and hear the flies coughing."

"Well," said Hans, "if she is not really wise, I won't have her."

When they were sitting at dinner and had eaten, the mother said, "Elsie, go into the cellar and fetch some beer."

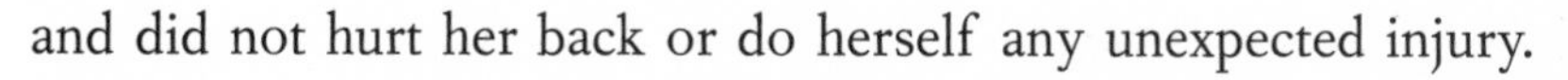

Then Clever Elsie took the pitcher from the wall, went into the cellar, and tapped the lid briskly as she went, so that the time might not appear long. When she was below, she fetched herself a chair and set it before the barrel so that she had no need to stoop and did not hurt her back or do herself any unexpected injury. Then she placed the can before her and turned the tap; and while the beer was running, she would not let her eyes be idle but looked up at the wall. And after much peering here and there, saw a pickaxe exactly above her, which the masons had accidentally left there.

Then Clever Elsie began to weep, and said, "If I get Hans, and we have a child, and he grows big, and we send him into the cellar here to draw beer, then the pickaxe will fall on his head and kill him." Then she sat and wept and screamed with all the strength of her body, over the misfortune which lay before her.

Those upstairs waited for the drink, but Clever Elsie still did not come. Then the woman said to the servant, "Just go down into the cellar and see where Elsie is."

The maid went and found her sitting in front of the barrel, screaming loudly. "Elsie, why weepest thou?" asked the maid.

"Ah," she answered, "have I not reason to weep? If I get Hans, and we have a child, and he grows big and has to draw beer here, the pickaxe will perhaps fall on his head and kill him."

Then said the maid, "What a clever Elsie we have!" And she sat down beside her and began loudly to weep over the misfortune.

After a while, as the maid did not come back and those upstairs were thirsty for the beer, the man said to the boy, "Just go down into the cellar and see where Elsie and the girl are."

The boy went down, and there sat Clever Elsie and the girl, both weeping together. Then he asked, "Why are ye weeping?"

"Ah," said Elsie, "have I not reason to weep? If I get Hans, and we have a child, and he grows big and has to draw beer here, the pickaxe will fall on his head and kill him."

Then said the boy, "What a clever Elsie we have!" And he sat down by her

and likewise began to howl loudly.

Upstairs they waited for the boy, but as he still did not return, the man said to the woman, "Just go down into the cellar and see where Elsie is!"

The woman went down, and found all three in the midst of their lamentations, and inquired what was the cause; then Elsie told her also that her future child was to be killed by the pickaxe, when he grew big and had to draw beer, and the pickaxe fell down. Then said the mother likewise, "What a clever Elsie we have!" And she sat down and wept with them.

The man upstairs waited a short time, but as his wife did not come back and his thirst grew ever greater, he said, "I must go into the cellar myself and see where Elsie is."

But when he got into the cellar, and they were all sitting together crying, and he heard the reason, and that Elsie's child was the cause, and that Elsie might perhaps bring one into the world someday and that he might be killed by the pickaxe, if he should happen to be sitting beneath it, drawing beer just at the very time when it fell down, he cried, "Oh, what a clever Elsie!" and sat down and likewise wept with them.

The bridegroom stayed upstairs alone for a long time; then as no one would come back, he thought, "They must be waiting for me below; I too must go there and see what they are about." When he got down, five of them were sitting, screaming and lamenting quite piteously, each outdoing the other. "What misfortune has happened then?" he asked.

"Ah, dear Hans," said Elsie, "if we marry each other and have a child, and he is big, and we perhaps send him here to draw something to drink, then the pickaxe which has been left up there might dash his brains out if it were to fall down, so have we not reason to weep?"

"Come," said Hans, "more understanding than that is not needed for my household, as thou art such a clever Elsie, I will have thee," and he seized her hand, took her upstairs with him, and married her.

After Hans had had her some time, he said, "Wife, I am going out to work and earn some money for us. Go into the field and cut the corn that we may have some bread."

"Yes, dear Hans, I will do that." After Hans had gone away, she cooked herself some good broth and took it into the field with her. When she came to the field she said to herself, "What shall I do? Shall I shear first, or shall I eat first? Oh, I will eat first." Then she emptied her basin of broth, and when she was fully satisfied, she once more said, "What shall I do? Shall I shear first, or shall I sleep first? I will sleep first." Then she lay down among the corn and fell asleep.

Hans had been at home for a long time, but Elsie did not come; then said he, "What a clever Elsie I have; she is so industrious that she does not even come home to eat." As, however, she still stayed away, and it was evening, Hans went out to see what she had cut, but nothing was cut, and she was lying among the corn, asleep. Then Hans hastened home and brought a fowler's net with little bells and hung it round about her, and she still went on sleeping. Then he ran home, shut the house-door, and sat down in his chair and worked.

At length, when it was quite dark, Clever Elsie awoke; and when she got up there was a jingling all round about her, and the bells rang at each step which she took. Then she was alarmed and became uncertain whether she really was Clever Elsie or not, and said, "Is it I, or is it not I?" But she knew not what answer to make to this, and stood for a time in doubt. At length she thought, "I will go home and ask if it be I, or if it be not I; they will be sure to know." She ran to the door of her own house, but it was shut; then she knocked at the window and cried, "Hans, is Elsie within?"

"Yes," answered Hans, "she is within."

Hereupon she was terrified, and said, "Ah, heavens! Then it is not I," and went to another door; but when the people heard the jingling of the bells they would not open it, and she could get in nowhere. Then she ran out of the village, and no one has seen her since.

# The Wishing Table, the Gold Ass, and the Cudgel in the Sack

HERE WAS ONCE A UPON A TIME A TAILOR WHO HAD three sons and only one goat. But as the goat supported the whole of them with her milk, she was obliged to have good food and to be taken every day to pasture. The sons, therefore, did this in turn.

Once the eldest took her to the churchyard, where the finest herbs were to be found, and let her eat and run about there. At night when it was time to go home he asked, "Goat, hast thou had enough?"

The goat answered,

*"I have eaten so much,*
*Not a leaf more I'll touch, meh! meh!"*

"Come home, then," said the youth, and took hold of the cord round her neck, led her into the stable, and tied her up securely.

"Well," said the old tailor, "has the goat had as much food as she ought?"

"Oh," answered the son, "she has eaten so much, not a leaf more she'll touch."

But the father wished to satisfy himself, and went down to the stable, stroked the dear animal, and asked, "Goat, art thou satisfied?"

The goat answered,

> *"Wherewithal should I be satisfied?*
> *Among the graves I leapt about,*
> *And found no food, so went without, meh! meh!"*

"What do I hear?" cried the tailor. And he ran upstairs and said to the youth, "Hollo, thou liar: thou saidest the goat had had enough, and hast let her hunger!" And in his anger he took the yard-measure from the wall, and drove him out with blows.

Next day it was the turn of the second son, who looked out for a place

in the fence of the garden, where nothing but good herbs grew, and the goat cleared them all off.

At night when he wanted to go home, he asked, "Goat, art thou satisfied?"

The goat answered,

*"I have eaten so much,*

*Not a leaf more I'll touch, meh! meh!"*

"Come home, then," said the youth, and led her home, and tied her up in the stable.

"Well," said the old tailor, "has the goat had as much food as she ought?"

"Oh," answered the son, "she has eaten so much, not a leaf more she'll touch."

The tailor would not rely on this, but went down to the stable and said, "Goat, hast thou had enough?"

The goat answered,

*"Wherewithal should I be satisfied?*

*Among the graves I leapt about,*

*And found no food, so went without, meh! meh!"*

"The godless wretch," cried the tailor, "to let such a good animal hunger!" And he ran up and drove the youth out of doors with the yard-measure.

Now came the turn of the third son, who wanted to do the thing well and sought out some bushes with the finest leaves and let the goat devour them. In the evening when he wanted to go home, he asked, "Goat, hast thou had enough?"

The goat answered,

*"I have eaten so much,*

*Not a leaf more I'll touch, meh! meh!"*

"Come home, then," said the youth, and led her into the stable and tied her up.

"Well," said the old tailor, "has the goat had a proper amount of food?"

"She has eaten so much, not a leaf more she'll touch."

The tailor did not trust to that, but went down and asked, "Goat, hast thou had enough?"

The wicked beast answered,

*"Wherewithal should I be satisfied?*
*Among the graves I leapt about,*
*And found no leaves, so went without, meh! meh!"*

"Oh, the brood of liars," cried the tailor, "each as wicked and forgetful of his duty as the other! Ye shall no longer make a fool of me," and quite beside himself with anger, he ran upstairs and belabored the poor young fellow so vigorously with the yard-measure that he sprang out of the house.

The old tailor was now alone with his goat. Next morning he went down into the stable, caressed the goat, and said, "Come, my dear little animal; I will take thee to feed myself." He took her by the rope and conducted her to green hedges, and amongst milfoil and whatever else goats like to eat. "There thou mayest for once eat to thy heart's content," said he to her, and let her browse till evening. Then he asked, "Goat, art thou satisfied?"

She replied,

*"I have eaten so much,*
*Not a leaf more I'll touch, meh! meh!"*

"Come home, then," said the tailor, and led her into the stable and tied her fast. When he was going away, he turned round again and said, "Well, art thou satisfied for once?"

But the goat did not behave the better to him, and cried,

*"Wherewithal should I be satisfied?*
*Among the graves I leapt about,*
*And found no leaves, so went without, meh! meh!"*

When the tailor heard that, he was shocked and saw clearly that he had driven away his three sons without cause. "Wait, thou ungrateful creature," cried he. "It is not enough to drive thee forth; I will mark thee so that thou wilt no more dare to show thyself amongst honest tailors." In great haste he ran upstairs, fetched his razor, lathered the goat's head, and shaved her as clean as the palm of his hand. And as the yard-measure would have been too good for her, he brought the horsewhip and gave her such cuts with it that she ran away in violent haste.

When the tailor was thus left quite alone in his house, he fell into great grief and would gladly have had his sons back again, but no one knew whither they were gone.

The eldest had apprenticed himself to a joiner and learnt industriously and indefatigably; and when the time came for him to go traveling, his master presented him with a little table which had no particular appearance and was made of common wood, but it had one good property: if anyone set it out and said, "Little table, spread thyself," the good little table was at once covered with a clean little cloth, and a plate was there and a knife and fork beside it, and dishes with boiled meats and roasted meats, as many as there was room for; and a great glass of red wine shone so that it made the heart glad. The young journeyman thought, "With this thou hast enough for thy whole life," and went joyously about the world and never troubled himself at all whether an inn was good or bad, or if anything was to be found in it or not. When it suited him, he did not enter an inn at all, but either on the plain, in a wood, a meadow, or wherever he fancied, he took his little table off his back, set it down before him, and said, "Cover thyself," and then everything appeared that his heart desired. At length he took it into his head to go back to his father, whose anger would now be appeased and who would now willingly receive him with his wishing table.

It came to pass that on his way home, he came one evening to an inn which was filled with guests. They bade him welcome, and invited him to sit and eat with them, for otherwise he would have difficulty in getting anything. "No," answered the joiner, "I will not take the few bites out of your mouths; rather than that, you shall be my guests." They laughed, and thought he was jesting with them; he, however, placed his wooden table in the middle of the room, and said, "Little table, cover thyself." Instantly it was covered with food, so good that the host could never have procured it, and the smell of it ascended pleasantly to the nostrils of the guests. "Fall to, dear friends," said the joiner; and the guests when they saw that he meant it, did not need to be asked twice but drew near, pulled out their knives, and attacked it valiantly. And what surprised them the most was that when a dish became empty, a full one instantly took its place of its own accord.

The innkeeper stood in one corner and watched the affair; he did not at all know what to say, but thought, "Thou couldst easily find a use for such a cook as that in thy kitchen." The joiner and his comrades made merry until late into the night; at length they lay down to sleep, and the young apprentice also went to bed, and set his magic table against the wall. The host's thoughts, however, let him have no rest. It occurred to him that there was a little old table in his lumber-room which looked just like the apprentice's; and he brought it out quite softly and exchanged it for the wishing table.

Next morning, the joiner paid for his bed, took up his table, never thinking that he had got a false one, and went his way. At mid-day he reached his father, who received him with great joy. "Well, my dear son, what hast thou learnt?" said he to him.

"Father, I have become a joiner."

"A good trade," replied the old man; "but what hast thou brought back with thee from thy apprenticeship?"

"Father, the best thing which I have brought back with me is this little table."

The tailor inspected it on all sides and said, "Thou didst not make a masterpiece when thou madest that; it is a bad old table."

"But it is a table which furnishes itself," replied the son. "When I set it out, and tell it to cover itself, the most beautiful dishes stand on it, and a wine also, which gladdens the heart. Just invite all our relations and friends; they shall refresh and enjoy themselves for once, for the table will give them all they require."

When the company was assembled, he put his table in the middle of the room and said, "Little table, cover thyself," but the little table did not bestir itself and remained just as bare as any other table which did not understand language. Then the poor apprentice became aware that his table had been changed, and was ashamed at having to stand there like a liar. The relations, however, mocked him, and were forced to go home without having eaten or drunk. The father brought out his patches again and went on tailoring, but the son went to a master in the craft.

The second son had gone to a miller and had apprenticed himself to him. When his years were over, the master said, "As thou hast conducted thyself so well, I give thee an ass of a peculiar kind, which neither draws a cart nor carries a sack."

"To what use is he put, then?" asked the young apprentice.

"He lets gold drop from his mouth," answered the miller. "If thou settest him on a cloth and sayest 'Bricklebrit,' the good animal will drop gold pieces for thee."

"That is a fine thing," said the apprentice, and thanked the master, and went out into the world.

When he had need of gold, he had only to say "Bricklebrit" to his ass, and it rained gold pieces, and he had nothing to do but pick them off the ground. Wheresoever he went, the best of everything was good enough for him, and the dearer the better, for he had always a full purse. When he had looked about the world for some time, he thought, "Thou must seek out thy father; if thou goest to him with the gold ass he will forget his anger and receive thee well."

It came to pass that he came to the same public house in which his brother's table had been exchanged. He led his ass by the bridle, and the host was about to take the animal from him and tie him up, but the young apprentice said, "Don't trouble yourself, I will take my grey horse into the stable and tie him up myself, too, for I must know where he stands." This struck the host as odd, and he thought that a man who was forced to look after his ass himself, could not have much to spend; but when the stranger put his hand in his pocket and brought out two gold pieces, and said he was to provide something good for him, the host opened his eyes wide and ran and sought out the best he could muster.

After dinner the guest asked what he owed. The host did not see why he should not double the reckoning, and said the apprentice must give two more gold pieces. He felt in his pocket, but his gold was just at an end. "Wait an instant, sir host," said he. "I will go and fetch some money"; but he took the tablecloth with him.

The host could not imagine what this could mean, and being curious, stole after him, and as the guest had bolted the stable-door, he peeped through a hole left by a knot in the wood. The stranger spread out the cloth under the animal and cried,

"Bricklebrit," and immediately the beast began to let gold pieces fall, so that it fairly rained down money on the ground.

"Eh, my word," said the host, "ducats are quickly coined there! A purse like that is not amiss." The guest paid his score and went to bed, but in the night the host stole down into the stable, led away the master of the mint, and tied up another ass in his place.

Early next morning the apprentice traveled away with his ass, and thought that he had his gold ass. At mid-day he reached his father, who rejoiced to see him again, and gladly took him in. "What hast thou made of thyself, my son?" asked the old man.

"A miller, dear father," he answered.

"What hast thou brought back with thee from thy travels?"

"Nothing else but an ass."

"There are asses enough here," said the father. "I would rather have had a good goat."

"Yes," replied the son, "but it is no common ass, but a gold ass, when I say 'Bricklebrit,' the good beast opens its mouth and drops a whole sheetful of gold pieces. Just summon all our relations hither, and I will make them rich folks."

"That suits me well," said the tailor, "for then I shall have no need to torment myself any longer with the needle," and ran out himself and called the relations together.

As soon as they were assembled, the miller bade them make way, spread out his cloth, and brought the ass into the room. "Now watch," said he, and cried, "Bricklebrit," but no gold pieces fell; and it was clear that the animal knew nothing of the art, for every ass does not attain such perfection. Then the poor miller pulled a long face, saw that he was betrayed, and begged pardon of the relatives, who went home as poor as they came.

There was no help for it: the old man had to betake him to his needle once more, and the youth hired himself to a miller.

The third brother had apprenticed himself to a turner, and as that is skilled labor, he was the longest in learning. His brothers, however, told him in a letter how badly things had gone with them, and how the innkeeper had cheated them of their beautiful wishing-gifts on the last evening before they reached home. When the turner had served his time, and had to set out on his travels, as he had conducted himself so well, his master presented him with a sack and said, "There is a cudgel in it."

"I can put on the sack," said he, "and it may be of good service to me, but why should the cudgel be in it? It only makes it heavy."

"I will tell thee why," replied the master. "If anyone has done anything to injure thee, do but say, 'Out of the sack, Cudgel!' and the cudgel will leap forth among the people and play such a dance on their backs that they will not be able to stir or move for a week; and it will not leave off until thou sayest, 'Into the sack, Cudgel!'"

The apprentice thanked him and put the sack on his back, and when anyone came too near him and wished to attack him, he said, "Out of the sack, Cudgel!" and instantly the cudgel sprang out and dusted the coat or jacket of one after the other on their backs and never stopped until it had stripped it off them; and it was done so quickly that before anyone was aware, it was already his own turn. In the evening the young turner reached the inn where his brothers had been cheated. He laid his sack on the table before him, and began to talk of all the wonderful things which he had seen in the world.

"Yes," said he, "people may easily find a table which will cover itself, a gold ass, and things of that kind—extremely good things which I by no means despise—but these are nothing in comparison with the treasure which I have won for myself and am carrying about with me in my sack there."

The innkeeper pricked up his ears. "What in the world can that be?" thought he. "The sack must be filled with nothing but jewels. I ought to get them cheap, too, for all good things go in threes."

When it was time for sleep, the guest stretched himself on the bench and laid his sack beneath him for a pillow. When the inn-keeper thought his guest was lying in a sound sleep, he went to him and pushed and pulled quite gently and carefully at the sack to see if he could possibly draw it away and lay another in its place. The turner had, however, been waiting for this for a long time; and now just as the inn-keeper was about to give a hearty tug, he cried, "Out of the sack, Cudgel!" Instantly the little cudgel came forth, and fell on the inn-keeper and gave him a sound thrashing.

The host cried for mercy;

but the louder he cried, so much more heavily the cudgel beat the time on his back, until at length he fell to the ground exhausted. Then the turner said, "If thou dost not give back the table which covers itself and the gold ass, the dance shall begin afresh."

"Oh, no," cried the host, quite humbly. "I will gladly produce everything, only make the accursed kobold creep back into the sack."

Then said the apprentice, "I will let mercy take the place of justice, but beware of getting into mischief again!" So he cried, "Into the sack, Cudgel!" and let him have rest.

Next morning the turner went home to his father with the wishing table and the gold ass. The tailor rejoiced when he saw him once more, and asked him likewise what he had learnt in foreign parts. "Dear father," said he, "I have become a turner."

"A skilled trade," said the father. "What hast thou brought back with thee from thy travels?"

"A precious thing, dear father," replied the son, "a cudgel in the sack."

"What!" cried the father. "A cudgel! That's worth thy trouble, indeed! From every tree thou can cut thyself one."

"But not one like this, dear father. If I say, 'Out of the sack, Cudgel!' the cudgel springs out and leads anyone who means ill with me a weary dance and never stops until he lies on the ground and prays for fair weather. Look you, with this cudgel have I got back the wishing table and the gold ass which the thievish inn-keeper took away from my brothers. Now let them both be sent for, and invite all our kinsmen. I will give them to eat and to drink, and will fill their pockets with gold into the bargain."

The old tailor would not quite believe, but nevertheless got the relatives together. Then the turner spread a cloth in the room and led in the gold ass, and said to his brother, "Now, dear brother, speak to him."

The miller said, "Bricklebrit," and instantly the gold pieces fell down on the cloth like a thunder-shower, and the ass did not stop until every one of them had so much that he could carry no more. (I can see in thy face that thou also wouldst like to be there.)

Then the turner brought the little table, and said, "Now, dear brother, speak to it."

And scarcely had the carpenter said, "Table, cover thyself," than it was spread and amply covered with the most exquisite dishes. Then such a meal took place as the good tailor had never yet known in his house, and the whole party of kinsmen stayed together till far in the night and were all merry and glad. The tailor locked away needle and thread, yard-measure and goose, in a press and lived with his three sons in joy and splendor.

What, however, has become of the goat who was to blame for the tailor driving out his three sons? That I will tell thee. She was ashamed that she had a bald head, and ran to a fox's hole and crept into it. When the fox came home, he was met by two great eyes shining out of the darkness, and was terrified and ran away. A bear met him, and as the fox looked quite disturbed, he said, "What is the matter with thee, brother fox? Why dost thou look like that?"

"Ah," answered Redskin, "a fierce beast is in my cave and stared at me with its fiery eyes."

"We will soon drive him out," said the bear, and went with him to the cave and looked in, but when he saw the fiery eyes, fear seized on him likewise. He would have nothing to do with the furious beast and took to his heels.

The bee met him, and as she saw that he was ill at ease, she said, "Bear, thou art really pulling a very pitiful face. What has become of all thy gaiety?"

"It is all very well for thee to talk," replied the bear. "A furious beast with staring eyes is in Redskin's house, and we can't drive him out."

The bee said, "Bear, I pity thee. I am a poor weak creature whom thou wouldst not turn aside to look at, but still, I believe, I can help thee." She flew into the fox's cave, lighted on the goat's smoothly shorn head, and stung her so violently, that she sprang up, crying, "Meh, meh," and ran forth into the world as if mad, and to this hour no one knows where she has gone.

# Thumbling

HERE WAS ONCE A POOR PEASANT WHO SAT IN THE evening by the hearth and poked the fire, and his wife sat and span. Then said he, "How sad it is that we have no children! With us all is so quiet, and in other houses it is noisy and lively."

"Yes," replied the wife, and sighed. "Even if we had only one, and it were quite small and only as big as a thumb, I should be quite satisfied, and we would still love it with all our hearts." Now it so happened that the woman fell ill, and after seven months gave birth to a child that was perfect in all its limbs, but no longer than a thumb.

Then, said they, "It is as we wished it to be, and it shall be our dear child"; and because of its size, they called it Thumbling. They did not let it want for food, but the child did not grow taller but remained as it had been at the first; nevertheless it looked sensibly out of its eyes, and soon showed itself to be a wise and nimble creature, for everything it did turned out well.

One day the peasant was getting ready to go into the forest to cut wood, when he said as if to himself, "How I wish that there was anyone who would bring the cart to me!"

"Oh, Father," cried Thumbling, "I will soon bring the cart, rely on that; it shall be in the forest at the appointed time."

The man smiled and said, "How can that be done? Thou art far too small to lead the horse by the reins?"

"That's of no consequence, Father. If my mother will only harness it, I shall sit in the horse's ear and call out to him how he is to go."

"Well," answered the man, "for once we will try it."

When the time came, the mother harnessed the horse and placed Thumbling in its ear; and then the little creature cried, "Gee up, gee up!"

Then it went quite properly as if with its master, and the cart went the right way into the forest. It so happened that just as he was turning a corner, and the little one was crying, "Gee up," two strange men came towards him.

"My word!" said one of them. "What is this? There is a cart coming, and a driver is calling to the horse, and still he is not to be seen!"

"That can't be right," said the other. "We will follow the cart and see where it stops."

The cart, however, drove right into the forest, and exactly to the place where the wood had been cut. When Thumbling saw his father, he cried to him, "Seest thou, Father, here I am with the cart; now take me down." The father got hold of the horse with his left hand and with the right took his little son out of the ear. Thumbling sat down quite merrily on a straw, but when the two strange men saw him, they did not know what to say for astonishment.

Then one of them took the other aside and said, "Hark, the little fellow would make our fortune if we exhibited him in a large town for money. We will buy him." They went to the peasant and said, "Sell us the little man. He shall be well treated with us."

"No," replied the father, "he is the apple of my eye, and all the money in the world cannot buy him from me."

Thumbling, however, when he heard of the bargain, had crept up the folds of his father's coat, placed himself on his shoulder, and whispered in his ear, "Father, do give me away. I will soon come back again." Then the father parted with him to the two men for a handsome bit of money.

"Where wilt thou sit?" they said to him.

"Oh just set me on the rim of your hat, and then I can walk backwards and forwards and look at the country and still not fall down."

They did as he wished, and when Thumbling had taken leave of his father, they went away with him. They walked until it was dusk, and then the little fellow said, "Do take me down, I want to come down." The man took his hat off and put the little fellow on the ground by the wayside; and he leapt and crept about a little between the sods, and then he suddenly slipped into a mousehole which he had sought out. "Good evening, gentlemen. Just go home without me," he cried to them and mocked them.

They ran thither and stuck their sticks into the mouse-hole, but it was all lost labor. Thumbling crept still farther in, and as it soon became quite dark, they were forced to go home with their vexation and their empty purses.

When Thumbling saw that they were gone, he crept back out of the subterranean passage. "It is so dangerous to walk on the ground in the dark," said he. "How easily a neck or a leg is broken!" Fortunately he knocked against an empty snail shell. "Thank God!" said he. "In that I can pass the night in safety," and got into it. Not long afterwards, when he was just going to sleep, he heard two men go by, and one of them was saying, "How shall we contrive to get hold of the rich pastor's silver and gold?"

"I could tell thee that," cried Thumbling, interrupting them.

"What was that?" said one of the thieves in fright. "I heard someone speaking."

They stood still listening, and Thumbling spoke again, and said, "Take me with you, and I'll help you."

"But where art thou?"

"Just look on the ground, and observe from whence my voice comes," he replied.

There the thieves at length found

him, and lifted him up. "Thou little imp, how wilt thou help us?" they said.

"A great deal," said he. "I will creep into the pastor's room through the iron bars, and will reach out to you whatever you want to have."

"Come then," they said, "and we will see what thou canst do."

When they got to the pastor's house, Thumbling crept into the room but instantly cried out with all his might, "Do you want to have everything that is here?"

The thieves were alarmed, and said, "But do speak softly, so as not to waken anyone!"

Thumbling, however, behaved as if he had not understood this, and cried again, "What do you want? Do you want to have everything that is here?"

The cook, who slept in the next room, heard this and sat up in bed, and listened. The thieves, however, had in their fright run some distance away, but at last they took courage, and thought, "The little rascal wants to mock us." They came back and whispered to him, "Come, be serious, and reach something out to us."

Then Thumbling again cried as loudly as he could, "I really will give you everything; just put your hands in."

The maid who was listening heard this quite distinctly and jumped out of bed and rushed to the door. The thieves took flight, and ran as if the Wild Huntsman were behind them, but as the maid could not see anything, she went to strike a light. When she came to the place with it, Thumbling, unperceived, betook himself to the granary, and the maid, after she had examined every corner and found nothing, lay down in her bed again and believed that, after all, she had only been dreaming with open eyes and ears. Thumbling had climbed up among the hay and found a beautiful place to sleep in; there he intended to rest until day, and then go home again to his parents. But he had other things to go through. Truly, there is much affliction and misery in this world!

When day dawned, the maid arose from her bed to feed the cows. Her first walk was into the barn, where she laid hold of an armful of hay, and precisely that very one in which poor Thumbling was lying asleep. He, however, was sleeping so soundly that he was aware of nothing and did not awake until he was in the mouth of the cow, who had picked him up with the hay. "Ah, heavens!" cried he. "How have I got into the fulling mill?" But he soon discovered where he was. Then it was necessary to be careful not to let himself go between the teeth and be dismembered, but he was nevertheless forced to slip down into the stomach with the hay. "In this little room the windows are forgotten," said he, "and no sun shines in, neither will a candle be brought." His quarters were especially unpleasing to him, and the worst was, more and more hay was always coming in by the door, and the space grew less and less. Then at length in his anguish, he cried as loud as he could, "Bring me no more fodder, bring me no more fodder."

The maid was just milking the cow, and when she heard someone speaking and saw no one and perceived that it was the same voice that she had heard in the night, she was so terrified that she slipped off her stool and spilt the milk. She ran in great haste to her master, and said, "Oh heavens, Pastor, the cow has been speaking!"

"Thou art mad," replied the pastor; but he went himself to the byre to see what was there.

Hardly, however had he set his foot inside when Thumbling again cried, "Bring me no more fodder, bring me no more fodder." Then the pastor himself was alarmed, and thought that an evil spirit had gone into the cow, and ordered her to be killed.

She was killed, but the stomach, in which Thumbling was, was thrown on the midden. Thumbling had great difficulty in working his way out; however, he succeeded so far as to get some room, but just as he was going to thrust his head out, a new misfortune occurred. A hungry wolf ran thither and swallowed the whole stomach at one gulp. Thumbling did not lose courage. "Perhaps," thought he, "the wolf will listen to what I have got to say." And he called to him from out of his stomach, "Dear wolf, I know of a magnificent feast for you."

"Where is it to be had?" said the wolf.

"In such and such a house. Thou must creep into it through the kitchen sink, and wilt find cakes and bacon and sausages, and as much of them as thou canst eat," and he described to him exactly his father's house. The wolf did not require to be told this twice, squeezed himself in at night through the sink, and ate to his heart's content in the larder. When he had eaten his fill, he wanted to go out again, but he had become so big that he could not go out by the same way. Thumbling had reckoned on this, and now began to make a violent noise in the wolf's body, and raged and screamed as loudly as he could.

"Wilt thou be quiet," said the wolf. "Thou wilt waken up the people!"

"Eh, what," replied the little fellow, "thou hast eaten thy fill, and I will make merry likewise," and began once more to scream with all his strength. At last his father and mother were aroused by it and ran to the room and looked in through the opening in the door. When they saw that a wolf was inside, they ran away, and the husband fetched his axe and the wife the scythe.

"Stay behind," said the man, when they entered the room. "When I have

given him a blow, if he is not killed by it, thou must cut him down and hew his body to pieces."

Then Thumbling heard his parents, voices and cried, "Dear father, I am here; I am in the wolf's body."

Said the father, full of joy, "Thank God, our dear child has found us again," and bade the woman take away her scythe that Thumbling might not be hurt with it. After that he raised his arm and struck the wolf such a blow on his head that he fell down dead, and then they got knives and scissors and cut his body open and drew the little fellow forth. "Ah," said the father, "what sorrow we have gone through for thy sake."

"Yes, Father, I have gone about the world a great deal. Thank heaven, I breathe fresh air again!"

"Where hast thou been, then?"

"Ah, Father, I have been in a mouse's hole, in a cow's stomach, and then in a wolf's; now I will stay with you."

"And we will not sell thee again, no, not for all the riches in the world," said his parents, and they embraced and kissed their dear Thumbling. They gave him things to eat and to drink, and had some new clothes made for him, for his own had been spoiled on his journey.

# The Wedding of Mrs. Fox

## ~ First Story ~

HERE WAS ONCE ON A TIME AN OLD FOX WITH NINE tails, who believed that his wife was not faithful to him and wished to try her. He stretched himself out under the bench, did not move a limb, and behaved as if he were stone dead. Mrs. Fox went up to her room, shut herself in, and her maid, Miss Cat, sat by the fire, and did the cooking. When it became known that the old fox was dead, wooers presented themselves.

The maid heard someone standing at the house-door, knocking. She went and opened it, and it was a young fox, who said,

"What may you be about, Miss Cat?
Do you sleep or do you wake?"

She answered,

"I am not sleeping, I am waking,
Wouldst thou know what I am making?
I am boiling warm beer with butter so nice,
Will the gentleman enter and drink some likewise?"

"No, thank you, miss," said the fox. "What is Mrs. Fox doing?"

The maid replied,

"She sits all alone,
And makes her moan,
Weeping her little eyes quite red,
Because old Mr. Fox is dead."

"Do just tell her, miss, that a young fox is here, who would like to woo her."

"Certainly, young sir."

The cat goes up the stairs trip, trap,
The door she knocks at tap, tap, tap,
"Mistress Fox, are you inside?"
"Oh yes, my little cat," she cried.
"A wooer he stands at the door out there."
"Tell me what he is like, my dear?"

"But has he nine as beautiful tails as the late Mr. Fox?"

"Oh, no," answered the cat, "he has only one."

"Then I will not have him."

Miss Cat went downstairs and sent the wooer away. Soon afterwards there was another knock, and another fox was at the door who wished to woo Mrs. Fox. He had two tails, but he did not fare better than the first. After this still more came, each with one tail more than the other, but they were all turned away, until at last one came who had nine tails, like old Mr. Fox. When the widow heard that, she said joyfully to the cat,

"Now open the gates and doors all wide,
And carry old Mr. Fox outside."

But just as the wedding was going to be solemnized, old Mr. Fox stirred under the bench, and cudgeled all the rabble, and drove them and Mrs. Fox out of the house.

## ~ Second Story ~

When old Mr. Fox was dead, the wolf came as a wooer and knocked at the door, and the cat who was servant to Mrs. Fox opened it for him. The wolf greeted her, and said,

"Good day, Mrs. Cat of Kehrewit,
How comes it that alone you sit?
What are you making good?"

The cat replied,

"In milk I'm breaking bread so sweet,
Will the gentleman please come in and eat?"

"No, thank you, Mrs. Cat," answered the wolf. "Is Mrs. Fox not at home?"

The cat said,

"She sits upstairs in her room,
Bewailing her sorrowful doom,
Bewailing her trouble so sore,
For old Mr. Fox is no more."

The wolf answered,

"If she's in want of a husband now,
Then will it please her to step below?"
The cat runs quickly up the stair,
And lets her tail fly here and there,
Until she comes to the parlor door.
With her five gold rings at the door she knocks,
"Are you within, good Mistress Fox?
If you're in want of a husband now,
Then will it please you to step below?

Mrs. Fox asked, "Has the gentleman red stockings on and has he a pointed mouth?"

"No," answered the cat.

"Then he won't do for me."

When the wolf was gone, came a dog, a stag, a hare, a bear, a lion, and all the beasts of the forest, one after the other. But one of the good points which old Mr. Fox had possessed was always lacking, and the cat had continually to send the wooers away.

At length came a young fox. Then Mrs. Fox said, "Has the gentleman red stockings on, and has he a little pointed mouth?"

"Yes," said the cat, "he has."

"Then let him come upstairs," said Mrs. Fox, and ordered the servant to prepare the wedding-feast.

"Sweep me the room as clean as you can,
Up with the window, fling out my old man!
For many a fine fat mouse he brought,
Yet of his wife he never thought,

But ate up every one he caught."

Then the wedding was solemnized with young Mr. Fox, and there was much rejoicing and dancing; and if they have not left off, they are dancing still.